FOR THY G
HAVE MERCY
ON MY
LITTLE PAIN

for thy great pain have mercy on my little pain

VICTORIA MACKENZIE

BLOOMSBURY PUBLISHING

LONDON · OXFORD · NEW YORK · NEW DELHI · SYDNEY

BLOOMSBURY PUBLISHING
Bloomsbury Publishing Plc
50 Bedford Square, London, WC1B 3DP, UK
29 Earlsfort Terrace, Dublin 2, Ireland

BLOOMSBURY, BLOOMSBURY PUBLISHING and the Diana logo are
trademarks of Bloomsbury Publishing Plc

First published in Great Britain, 2023

A catalogue record for this book is available from the British Library

ISBN: HB: 978-1-5266-4788-7; TPB: 978-1-5266-4787-0;
EPUB: 978-1-5266-4789-4; EPDF: 978-1-5266-4791-7

2 4 6 8 10 9 7 5 3 1

Typeset by Integra Software Services Pvt. Ltd.
Printed and bound in Great Britain by CPI Group (UK) Ltd, Croydon CR0 4YY

To find out more about our authors and books visit www.bloomsbury.com
and sign up for our newsletters

CONTENTS

For Garry and Struan, my beloved anchors.

And in happy memory of Patricia Sheath (1935–2022),
who made all things well.

Botte for I am a woman, schulde I therefore leve
that I schulde nought telle yowe the goodness of God?
Julian of Norwich, *Revelations of Divine Love*

Jesus, what shall I think about?
Margery Kempe, *The Book of Margery Kempe*

AUTHOR'S NOTE

This is a work of fiction, but one that is closely based on the lives of two women who lived in the late fourteenth and early fifteenth centuries. *For Thy Great Pain Have Mercy On My Little Pain* draws on B. A. Windeatt's translation of *The Book of Margery Kempe* and Elizabeth Spearing's translation of *Revelations of Divine Love* by Julian of Norwich. This work is a creative engagement with both texts as well as a work of imagination.

PROLOGUE

I fear that my neighbours are right, that it is the devil inside me, making me think that I see Christ.

Master Aleyn, my friend the Carmelite monk, said to me, 'Margery, you must go to Norwich to see the anchoress and hear her counsel.' But now I am here I wish I was back in Lynn. The streets are crowded and both men and women use foul curses. I saw a man put a live mouse between his lips as if it were the sacred host, cheered on by a group of sailors. I tutted as I passed them and one of the men called out to me as if I were a strumpet.

My maidservant has found us an inn, but it is not a comfortable place. I sit on the filthy bed and think I have never felt more wretched. For the first time in many years I wish I was at home with my children.

But this is my last hope. The devil won't have my soul. The anchoress will surely help me.

PART ONE

THE SHEWINGS

JULIAN

When I was a child of seven summers, a great pestilence
came to our city. As the death carts went up and down
the streets, the sound of their wheels and the horses'
hooves mingled with the sounds of weeping. But there
was little time for ceremony. *Thump.* The bodies were
wrapped in whatever was to hand — sheets, table-cloths,
rugs — and heaved on to the cart. I watched from an
upstairs window, something both my mother and my
nurse Joan had told me not to do. *Thump.* The cart trun-
dled to the next house. *Thump.* Sometimes a covering
came loose as a body hit the wooden planks, unravelling
to reveal a chin or an ear.

We were rich, this had always been clear to me. We ate
well and our house had many rooms. My clothes were
made from Flanders linen, and my mother had a garden
just for flowers. Just for beauty. Imagine. But still we died.

The pestilence travelled through the air, like the fog from the river that curled its way under our door in autumn. My father died, and my nurse Joan died, and my older brother William died. Then my younger sister Elizabeth died, whom I had always called Bethy. *Thump*. Her sweet, plump body was thrown away.

The city stank of rotting flesh. I was not allowed to play outside. There were no merchants, no boats and no markets that year; no crops were planted and no animals were herded through the city gates for slaughter. Even the bells fell silent.

Afterwards, my mother and I lived together in a more sombre way. She withdrew into sadness, rarely raising her eyes to me. I learnt to keep my own company, wandering through the empty rooms of the now too-big house, tiptoeing so I didn't disturb her. The flowers in her garden still bloomed, but my mother no longer tended them.

MARGERY

Christ first visited me some months after the birth of my eldest child, when I laboured for more hours than a single day can hold.

I suffered much when I was with child, with vomiting and aches, and I was afraid it was punishment for my sins. I also desired to eat strange things: clods of mud and leather soles from boots. My husband wasn't pleased and told me not to eat these things. He said that if I didn't stop, he would have me imprisoned in my chamber and he would put shackles on my arms.

At that, I quite lost my reason. I ranted and screamed and tore at my clothes and hair. And I was indeed restrained as my husband had threatened, and he took away my keys. Then my labour pains began and they were shackles themselves, pinning me down and causing me to roar.

My neighbour, Agnes, was at my side, to aid me through the birth, but she tutted at my cries and spent more time gossiping outside my room than rubbing my belly with rose oil.

When the child emerged I thought he was the devil come to split me in two and toss my entrails to the dogs. I prayed to St Margaret to relieve me of the terror and let me die quickly, but she did not hear my pleas. When Agnes pulled the devil from between my damp thighs, he brought other demons who pawed at me and hauled me about the bed all night and day.

I named the baby John, after his father, and Agnes cut the cord and swaddled him. The child was baptised at church two days later, but I could not leave my bed. The demons told me to forsake my faith and my husband and my friends, which I did, slandering them and recognising no goodness in them. They also told me to hurt myself and I scratched at my arms and made them bleed, and I bit my own hand very hard. Agnes put honey on the wound and bound it, but the mark has stayed ever since.

I believed I was dying and because of this I asked to see my confessor so I could tell him of a sin that had long been on my mind. I had never confessed it before because every time I thought to, something would whisper in my ear that if I repented in my mind and made penance, that was enough. I often did penance by fasting on bread and water and spending many hours at prayer. But now, when I thought I would die, I knew I must confess and be rid of the sin, or I could never lift my face to the Lord and receive his love.

My confessor came to my room and I said I wanted to be shriven of the sins of my whole life, so I began with the first sins of my childhood (including envy of my brother), up to the particular sin that was bothering me, but as I began to tell of this sin, my confessor was sharp with me, telling me not to take all day, and then I could not get the sin out. This made me frenzied and I hurt myself more.

It was after this that Jesus Christ appeared, sitting on the edge of my bed, very handsome and clad in a mantle of purple silk. He looked at me with so blessed a countenance that I felt my spirit strengthen. He said, 'Daughter, why have you forsaken me, when I never forsook you?'

As soon as he said this, the air in my chamber became bright as if lit by lightning and he ascended to heaven, not rushing, but beautifully and slowly, until the air closed up again and I was restored to myself. After this everyone was most amazed at how I had recovered my wits and my husband gave me back my keys.

When I told my husband what I'd seen, he shook his head and said, 'Hush your mouth, wife, you're clucking like a silly goose.'

JULIAN

When I was nineteen years of age and married, living in the golden mist of my first child, the pestilence returned to our city, slinking through the streets, snuffing out life. Both my husband and baby died, yet death's shadow passed over me once more. For a long time I wished I were dead.

I didn't marry again, but returned to my mother's house, where we lived just the two of us. After about ten years, when I was thirty, I became very ill. For three nights I lay on my bed whilst fire and ice swept through me. On the fourth day, the priest put his fat thumb on my brow and I felt cold oil slip into my ear. My mother's finger closed my eyelids and in this way I knew I was not expected to live.

But then, without opening my eyes, I saw the priest's crucifix before me. I stared at the face of Our Lord and the crown of thorns that cut into his head. I stared at the painted blood that ran down his cheeks. But it was not paint: he was a living man, with hot blood pouring from his wounds. This was the first of my *shewings*.

MARGERY

When I told my neighbours that Christ had shown himself to me, they laughed. 'Why would he show himself to a woman?' they said. 'Do kings speak to you also? Does the Pope creep into your room at night and whisper things only for your special sacred ears? Ha!'

My cheeks glowed, as if the flames of hell were near. I knew that my vision of Jesus sitting on my bed was true and had come from heaven, but small doubts crept in like mice and nibbled at my certainty. What if my vision was from the devil? How could I be sure that my vision was something good and holy, and not something evil to make me look a fool?

I felt full of shame after this and didn't speak of my vision for a while. Instead, I took comfort by wearing a hair shirt in secret. It was itchier than I'd imagined, and sitting in church without scratching was a great trial. I also made small lacerations in my arms, which seemed to ease the shame I felt. I prayed with nettle leaves crushed in my palms, and placed a stone in my shoe like a pilgrim, though I took it out when I got a blister the size of a gooseberry.

JULIAN

I did not speak of my *shewings* to anyone. I wanted time to think upon them, but I also knew that they would not be well received. My priest, Master Walter, had often spoken about the dangers of heresy. He said that those whose beliefs strayed from the teachings of the Holy Church would be damned. The word *heresy* rested heavy on my heart.

Instead, I wrote my *shewings* down in secret as soon as I felt well enough. I wondered why God had chosen me and what he wanted of me. I wondered if I was meant to change my life in some way and dedicate myself to him.

Some years later, after my mother's death, I chose to become an anchoress and I came to live in this cell. It is attached to St Julian's Church, the church I attended as a child, as a wife and mother, and then as a widow. I gave up my name and took the name of Julian.

I have not left this cell for twenty-three years.

I may not leave this cell, on pain of excommunication.

I will die in this cell and my bones will be interred beneath the floor.

MARGERY

Although my neighbours had laughed at me about my vision, I had a friend in the person of Master Aleyn, a Carmelite monk. I had been visiting him ever since I got married and he read to me from the Bible and *The Mirror of Simple Souls* by Marguerite Porete (she who was wrongly burnt as a heretic), as well as from the lives of other holy persons such as Bridget of Sweden, who died the year that I was born.

I told Master Aleyn about my vision of Jesus. 'Be careful, Margery,' he said. 'Some people say that those who claim direct contact with God are heretics.'

JULIAN

My cell has three flint walls and a low thatched roof and it clings like a limpet to the side of the church. There are three windows: one is narrow and cruciform, and looks directly into the church so I may take part in every mass and holy festival, make my confession and receive Christ's body and blood. From this window I glimpse the high altar and its candle, which is oftentimes my only light. The smell of the incense comes boldly into my cell, as does the rustle of the worshippers as they kneel and sit and stand. For keeping the hour, the bell is loud and inescapable.

A second window connects my cell with my maid's room, with a white linen curtain to hide our faces from each other.

A third window looks out on to King Street, a busy thoroughfare leading to the riverside docks. Hundreds of people walk down this street every day, so in this way I am still part of the world.

Before taking my vows I familiarised myself with the rules for anchoresses in the *Ancrene Wisse*. I wear no hair-shirts or hedgehog skins, and endure no whippings with holly or brambles. My clothes are plain but warm, and my shoes are leather and well made. I fast at Lenten, but otherwise my food is nourishing – bread, porridge and ale, with wine on feast days. My bed is a rush mat with a wool blanket and my arm is my pillow.

I have a small fire, but in winter my cell is cold. In summer my cell stays cool and I smell the river's reek.

Much of my day is given to prayer. I have grown stiff with kneeling till it is now quite an effort to haul myself up. But I am careful not to suffer. The life of an anchoress should be one of quiet reflection, not pain or self-denial. Indeed, it even has its pleasures. Within the confines of my cell I spend my time as I wish: in thought and prayer and writing. Not many women can make such a claim.

I am not entirely alone. My maid, Sara, passes everything I need through the window between our chambers. There is a sill where she places food and water, firewood, linen and thread. On this sill I place my slops and ashes. We are careful never to touch, for the *Ancrene Wisse* says that for another's hand to penetrate the cell is sinful.

Sara goes to market and she visits her family, but otherwise she is always near me, breathing quietly in the next room. Her ways of moving and speaking are as familiar to me as my own. I have never looked upon her face, but we have grown older together. She has never married but has dedicated her life to God just as I have, through her tender care of my person.

I have always had much to think about. When I entered my cell all those years ago, there were questions I wanted to dwell upon in peace, away from the fussing, brutal, chafing world:

How can we truly know God?

How can we best live, when the world is full of grief and suffering?

What is sin? Why should we, beloved of God, be free to sin, free to scorn his love – and thus *damn* ourselves for all eternity?

These are not insignificant questions; when I entered my cell I knew they would occupy me for many years.

MARGERY

If you are accused of heresy there are interrogations, and if they do not like your answers they burn you to death. I know this very well because it happened to William Sawtre, the priest of my own church, some years ago. He told us that if we could read the Bible for ourselves, we would need no priest. He also said that the Bible described no hot and fiery hell. He was declared a Lollard and taken to Smithfield for burning, his own fiery hell on earth.

I do not want to burn, not in this life or the next. I imagine how my clothes and hair would scorch first, and I'd be naked and bald, cooking for all the world to see. I imagine the meat of myself sizzling, the fat of my breasts and belly spitting, the skin of my arms crisping. How long until my tongue burnt off and I could no longer scream?

But I am not a heretic and I trust to God I will not be misjudged.

JULIAN

I have always been good at being quiet.

At being still.

Amidst the bustle of this world, it does no harm to have a woman who watches,

who sees the new leaves unfurl
the clouds build and darken and fall
the dewdrops gathering on the blades of grass
at dusk.

No one can enter my cell, but many people come to my window on King Street. When I have a visitor I put up a black curtain so my person is kept hidden. My visitors include lords and ladies, merchants and their wives, traders, farmers, weavers, dyers, bakers, coopers, tanners and women who sell their bodies. I give the same counsel to them all, reassuring them of God's love and asking them to find forgiveness and patience in their hearts for others. For we are all imperfect creatures, in need of these things daily.

From my window I hear many tongues – English, French, Latin, Flemish, Cornish – though laughter and anger sound much the same in any language. I hear dogs barking and horses whinnying, and the sound of traders calling out their wares has become as familiar as birdsong: *Hot peascods! Ribs of beef! Hot pies!*

From the mouths of pedlars and minstrels much information has reached my ears. I heard about the crowning of the new king, whose mother tongue was English, not French; I heard when there were three popes claiming to be the only true pope; I heard when Henry le Despenser died and the new bishop was consecrated; I heard when the poet Geoffrey Chaucer died.

I also hear much in the way of gossip and speculation. People tell me the stories of their lives, and some days my mind swirls with their words. Whispers of dark deeds and crimes and violence.

Some years ago they started burning heretics nearby. I'm told they're tied to stakes, with brushwood piled around them so the fire burns vigorously. When the wind blows from the north, I smell charred flesh on the breeze and hear screaming. I picture black petals of skin rising up into the air.

Heretics. That's what they call people who own a Bible in English; or who believe that men are saved through God's love; or who feel close to God without need of a priest to intercede for them; or who question whether the buying of pardons is really God's will. All over the city, houses are searched, people are arrested. The smell of burnt flesh hangs over the city, shaming it.

Go, gentle souls, I whisper over the screams. Depart this world and go to your Lord who loves you.

Sara tells me that weeping relatives sometimes beg for a remnant from among the ashes. The officials refuse, so loved ones come later, in secret, scrabbling for some piece of their departed, some chip of bone they can bury and visit as a grave.

After all these years, I have told no one of my *shewings*. People come to me because I am an anchoress and live quietly, not because I have heard the voice of God. I try to listen and to ease each heart that comes to me. People ask me to pray for them, and this I do with love and fervour. Some want me to be their confessor but I tell them they must speak to a priest, for I cannot absolve them. Bands of pilgrims visit too, on their way to take a boat to France. Some people bring me things, but I keep only what is of little value; the rest I give to the church. I have a shelf laden with pebbles, shells, feathers and dried flowers – if people ask for a memento, I give them an item from this shelf.

Occasionally, people ask me to look after things for them – money or jewels that they fear will be stolen by a drunken husband or an untrustworthy daughter. But I do not offer this service. Nor will I engage in any teaching or regular counsel, for if I did, I would have no time for prayer or meditation. Indeed, I have so many visitors it sometimes feels I do not have enough time for these things anyway. I must strive to keep my thoughts focused inwards, while the world is always trying to draw them outwards.

The *Ancrene Wisse* states that anchoresses may keep no animal but a cat. I have had several cats over the years, and they come and go from my cell as they please, without fear of excommunication. Indeed, my present cat fears nothing. I often joke with him, ask him if he has been visiting witches. We keep this joke to ourselves, lest we're overheard and both of us drowned or burnt.

But other creatures choose to share my cell: spiders, beetles, woodlice, earwigs, wasps, fleas, lice. One particularly cold year, a squirrel spent the winter under my bed. My cat did not approve and slept in Sara's room.

The street can be noisy at night with music, singing and shouting. There are taverns nearby, and occasionally men come to my window to abuse me. Once, a man threw a piece of stale bread into my window. Sara was woken by the sound and rushed out, waving her broom, but the man ran off before she could inflict her wrath upon him.

Although I do not speak of my *shewings*, there have been times when I wondered if it was God's will that I should. A man came to my window who whispered that what he was most afraid of was that there was no God: that the words of the mass were just old, dead words; that the bread the priest gave him was the same thing he ate at home; that the wine was nothing but fermented grapes. That all our living and dying was for no purpose; that we were just like the flies that hatch in the dung-clogged streets.

I had never met a soul so lacking in hope. I told him not to fear, that God was real and full of love for him. He asked me how I could be sure. I wanted to say it was because I had seen God and knew he was in all things, but he might have told someone of my claims.

Sometimes I wonder that people think me wise. Perhaps I am only a coward, scribbling in secret, allowing the stone walls of my cell to protect me from life's rough winds, like a snail's shell protects its damp muscle of flesh.

I often think of the man who feared God was not real. His soul was hungry, and to this day I fear I let him down, that I had spiritual food to offer but held back to protect myself.

MARGERY

I am from a good family of merchants in Bishop's Lynn, very good indeed, although not, I admit, quite of noble or royal connection. My father – still alive, praise God, but old – is a fine man. John Brunham was five times mayor of Lynn and twice a Member of Parliament. He has been a juror, a coroner and is in all ways highly respected in the town. He loves me dearly, as I him. He gave me my first horse, a dappled mare named Melody, and taught me to ride. He bought me fine robes and fur-trimmed cloaks, as well as jewellery and all the trinkets a young girl fancies. He gave me a Prayer Book, which I used to hold open as I walked to church, repeating the words from memory, pretending that I could read. Our church was St Margaret's, the grandest in Lynn, which I still attend. It has two enormous towers and a very grand chancel, and it must be one of the best churches in all of Christendom.

My mother paid me little notice, always busy with needlework and babies, content to sit at home and coo like an over-fed dove. None of these treasured children survived more than a few years, except my younger brother Ralph, my mother's favourite. But I didn't suffer from a lack of love because I had my father. Often he said to me, 'You should have been a boy, Marge. You'd have done fine things and made me proud. Become Mayor of Lynn yourself, perhaps.'

But as I grew up, my father spent more time with Ralph, teaching him business and laughing and joking with him in the way men do. When they discussed business matters I sat like a stone, hoping I would be allowed to stay in the room, but Ralph saw me and scowled, so my father sent me away, saying I should sit with my mother and practise my sewing.

Church became a comfort to me then. I attended mass every day and our neighbours praised my dutifulness. I enjoyed praying, moving the wooden beads of my rosary round and round until I had said hundreds of Ave Marias and paternosters. I liked fasting too, it made me feel clean inside. My stomach growled and I felt weak and I thought about the Lord on the cross and his agonies.

But when I grew into a woman, I hated my woman's body. My breasts were large and full, my hips wide, and men stared at me in the street. And when my monthly bleeding began – oh, I thought I would die from shame. My mother showed me how to roll strips of linen and push them inside myself, but all the while I was crying and telling her it couldn't be true that women had to do this.

'Get pregnant and you'll have some respite from this misery,' she said. 'Although then there'll be fresh misery to keep you busy.'

Every time my bleeding comes, I wish that I were not a woman.

My father noticed my changing body and remarked that he would be finding me a husband soon. I begged him not to. I said I would rather live with him and help him in any way I could.

'Margy,' he chuckled. 'I've got your mother. What would I be wanting with another woman about the place, nagging me to take my boots off and wanting money for a new tippet? No, my girl. You'll get a husband of your own, and you can bother *him* for tippet money.'

At this, I despaired I had ever asked my father for a new tippet.

To my surprise, my father let me remain at home for a few more years. He was busy with being Mayor and then a Member of Parliament. In this way I grew to be nineteen, and even *I* began to worry I would never be a wife. So when John Kempe was invited to dinner and afterwards my father said 'Well?', I nodded, even though

John Kempe was unlike his name and *unkempt*, having a tear in his sleeve and hair that flopped around.

John Kempe was also from a merchant family in Lynn, though not as successful or as well thought of as the Brunhams. But he was respectable enough – my father did not throw me away – and he pleased me well with his wedding gift: a rosary made from amber which he had obtained from a Danzig merchant, much finer than any I already owned.

Since then, however, my husband, though gentle and even-tempered, has proven himself a fool in business.

JULIAN

From my window I can see a hazel tree in the church-yard, the brick wall of a warehouse across the street, and a patch of sky beyond. Although I can no longer see the city, I can remember what's out there well enough. In my mind, I follow King Street down to the River Wensum where there are ships of all sizes, bringing goods and merchants and pilgrims and news and ideas.

As a child I walked past the docks on my daily walk. I saw barrels of salted herring, and boxes full of seeds and spices, and cobweb-fine Flemish lace. I saw brightly coloured birds that twittered and, once, a white bear. It was taller than a man, and its great paws thrashed at its wooden cage, sending splinters flying.

My nurse Joan always tried to drag me away, but I used to stare until my eyes ached. When I returned home I could remember much of what I had seen and enjoy it all again, as if it was there before me. Now, when I cannot leave my cell, this practice serves me well. I conjure in my mind the sights and sounds and smells I have not experienced in many years. I admit that sometimes I think I would like to see the water slapping at the wooden planks of the dock, or the tarred hulls of the largest ships, sails flapping with impatience for the next voyage. When I smell the scent of adventure that comes off the sea-faring folk as they pass my window, a strange feeling enters me, like grief or loss.

I have an alms box by my window, and visitors usually drop in a few coins in exchange for my counsel and prayers. Local women bring loaves and bags of wind-fall pears and firkins of new ale. At first Sara took offence at such gifts, as if they were a criticism of her skills, but I said we should be grateful that the people think of us.

Sara sneers at some of my visitors, telling me that they sit there picking lice off themselves while they talk to me, or that they wipe their noses on their sleeves, or scratch their behinds. I try not to laugh, but offer gentle words to her about the need for compassion. None of us live as angels.

MARGERY

Soon after my marriage, a travelling preacher told me that I was a sinner and must repent – that I must scourge my soul through mortification and penance, else God would show me no mercy. The preacher was talking to a group of people gathered around him, but as he spoke these words, he looked directly at me. And I knew he meant his words for me alone, that he could see all the sin in my heart, rotting me on the inside.

For though I tried to be good, somehow sin always overpowered me. I thought unkind thoughts about my brother, even after I was married and saw him less, and I took pride in wearing the most fashionable clothes. Over my hair shirt I still wore my favourite cloaks, with slashes to show the bright colours of my silk robes underneath. I was also argumentative with John, because whenever my husband suggested I leave off my proud ways, I would answer him that I was from a worthy family — if he did not like my ways, he should never have married me.

I also went to church during my unclean times, and sometimes I even had lustful thoughts about my husband. These sins weighed heavily on me, and I feared everyone could see my weakness.

When Christ came to me the first time, it was just a brief visit, but later he visited me many times, sometimes at church and sometimes in my bedchamber, and we talked for hours. He said to me, 'When you are in bed, you may boldly take me to you as your wedded husband. You can take me in the arms of your soul and kiss my mouth, my head and feet as sweetly as you want.' He took my hand and I tried to hide the scar where I had bitten myself after the birth of my first child, but he kissed the mark and said I did not need to feel shame in front of him.

When I told my husband what Jesus had said, he said that if he ever found me in bed with another man he'd cut off my nose. And that I should keep quiet about these so-called visions, because nobody liked a liar.

I told my neighbour, Agnes, that Jesus had visited me again. She looked at me as if I was speaking in riddles, and started talking about the weather.

During one of our holy conversations, Jesus asked me why I hadn't told any clerics about my visions. So I went to my priest, Master Hugh, and asked him if I could speak with him for an hour or two in the afternoon. He raised his hands and said, 'Bless us! What could a woman have to say about the Lord that could take so long?'

So I told him that Christ was coming before me. Master Hugh looked hard at me then, and when he spoke there was white spittle at the corners of his mouth. He said that only priests dealt directly with God, and to say otherwise made me a heretic.

'Jesus speaks to me in my soul,' I persisted. 'And I call these visions the *sight of my soul* because I do not see Christ with my eyes or hear him with my ears, but directly in my mind.'

'That's just your own sin talking,' he snapped.

'Jesus says that a lot of wickedness hides under the habit of holiness.'

Then Master Hugh gripped my neck and spoke closer, his breath smelling of wine. Flecks of spittle flew on to my cheek. He said that if I didn't shut my mouth he would have me arrested and he would see to it person-ally that I was burnt to death, for I was a troublesome woman who had never learnt to keep her place.

I knew then that he was not a man with the ear of God, no matter that he stood at the front of the church and told us what God thought of us.

When he let me go, I did not reply, but walked out of the church with my head held high.

That evening, I told my husband that Master Hugh had threatened me. He rolled his eyes like an ox. 'What did you expect, wife?' he said. 'That he would raise you as a saint? For God's sake, hold your tongue.'

But the next time I spoke with Our Lord in my soul, he said that he had no liking for Master Hugh, and if he spoke against me, then he was speaking against God, and therefore I was to pay no heed.

JULIAN

When I was a child and death swept away my siblings, at first I envied them. I envied them their deaths because I could see how my mother had loved them.

And though I was still near her, she did not seem to love me. But this was a child's perception and I was wrong. She always loved me and in time was able to show it again.

I became a very pestering child, always asking my mother if I could learn to read and write. She would answer 'O difficult child!' but say it smiling.

I don't know where I got this notion about reading from. Perhaps wandering into my dead brother William's room, touching his pen and papers, sitting where he had studied with his tutor. I opened his books and tried to scratch some marks with one of his pens but the inkpot was dry.

One afternoon, my mother found me asleep at William's desk, a pen clasped in my fingers. She kissed my hair and said, 'Very well.'

She asked the youngest son of a good family to teach me. His name was Simon and he was recently back from fighting in France.

'English only,' she admonished him. 'No Latin, or she'll ask to be a priest next.'

Simon was bemused by my delight in shaping letters. At first they were just patterns of nonsense, but slowly they swam into view as words. He sat beside me at the table, one leg stretched out before him. He had been lamed on the battlefield – sliced behind the knee with an axe.

'Why were you fighting in France?' I asked him. He smiled ruefully. 'I wish I knew.'

My mother didn't want to hear about my lessons, and said that if she ever saw me with inky fingers she'd whip me. I scrubbed them well and tried in every way to be a good daughter. I tended her garden, though she did not visit it, and I learnt how to make the flowers grow.

My mother had planted hollyhocks and peonies, marguerites and blue columbine for colour, and an orchard with pear and plum trees. In spring the blossom fell like white stars on the grass. I added juniper and bay for scent, and an herber, with lavender, angelica, catmint, lemon balm and marjoram.

And I discovered, as I raked and weeded and watered, that my thoughts often turned to God. He was in the air I breathed, in the soft leaves that sprouted, and even in the shiny beetles that scurried from my fingers.

I watched the other creatures that lived in the garden and I sat quietly to gain their trust – the robin and the thrush, the hedgehog and the bulging toad. I learnt that they had their own lives, and that God was in them too, and that all things God made were good, even the slugs which, though they ate my flowers, were food for the toad.

When I had mastered reading and writing a few words, I begged Simon not to tell my mother – for a few words were all she had permitted. I asked him to keep teaching me. He said he wouldn't lie to my mother, who was a good woman, but if she didn't ask then he wouldn't tell.

My learning continued for two years, during which time I read many texts that Simon lent me. I read Walter Hilton's *The Scale of Perfection*, addressed to a woman recently enclosed as an anchoress; and Rolle's *Incendium Amoris* in English; and other books that spoke about God's love. I copied out excerpts that I might re-read them and think upon them longer. One was from Hilton:

> *It had been a little purchase to Him to have come from so far to so near, and from so high to so low, for so few souls. Nay, His mercy is spread larger than so.*

I understood this to mean that Hilton did not believe most people would be damned. This was an intriguing idea that I gave much thought to.

As I became a better student, my lessons with Simon became more relaxed and we talked of other things. He spoke to me about his time in France, the fear he'd felt, and the pain when his knee was axed. I told him about my garden and the creatures that lived there.

My lessons stopped when Simon's father sent him north to oversee the running of a family estate. He was away for five years and I often thought of him during that time: his kindness, his smile, the gentle way he put the pen between my finger and thumb, guiding those first shaky marks.

MARGERY

Soon I had more babies, red and mewling, because my husband could not leave me alone. Every time I gave birth I smelt hot meat and shit, and wondered if it was the devil coming out of me.

Many times I told John that I wished for a chaste marriage, for I would have rather drunk the ooze in the gutter than lie with him any more. But he insisted on his rights.

When I saw young girls playing together under the shade of a tree, I wished I could be among them, whole and clean again.

JULIAN

There came a time that I was restless in my skin. My mother stared at me as though she'd never seen me before and, for no reason that I understood, I blushed.

'You'll be needing a husband,' she said.

I was aghast. Of course, I'd always known that marriage and motherhood lay in wait, but I'd hoped for a few more years of freedom yet.

I wondered if my future husband would be gruff and bearded, like my father, or a callow youth, fond of ale and dancing.

Then I thought perhaps I could become a nun. I could tend the *hortus conclusus* and use my writing skills to keep records in the convent. I began to pray a great deal.

'Why do you pray so much?' my mother asked.

'I pray until God is near me,' I said.

'You *summon* him?'

'No, God is always there. I pray until I can perceive him.'

I wanted to be as humble as a button, though I feared the very wish was not a humble thing. I wanted to be as innocent as a shaft of sunlight moving across the floor. For what shame does a shaft of sunlight feel?

I was lost and preoccupied with myself for a time. I am ashamed to say I became argumentative with my mother, and the atmosphere between us darkened.

'A house with two mistresses is never a happy home,' she observed.

We visited Yarmouth together, hoping that a change of air would bring a little tenderness between us. 'Look, daughter,' my mother said. 'The sea has much to say but she never contradicts, never argues, never disobeys.'

I hung my head and begged forgiveness. I kissed her hand and let my tears fall on her skin.

'Never mind,' she said. 'When you are married, we will be friends again.'

At this I turned away from her.

Now, in my cell, I let my soul wander to the coast again. I hear the soft sighing of the water. I see the light on the water. Small waves roll in, the colours changing from blue to grey to green. Gulls speckle the sky and a light mist soaks my hair.

O my speckled soul.

MARGERY

One night, as I was lying in bed with my husband, I heard the sweetest melody it was possible to hear, and I knew that I was hearing the music of heaven.

'Alas, that I ever sinned,' I called out. 'It is very merry in heaven!'

'What?' my husband mumbled, pulling the blanket over his head. 'Go to sleep, woman.'

'Don't you hear the music?' I asked him. 'I hear heaven, and it's the most joyous sound I ever heard!'

He didn't reply and soon began to snore. I knew he was truly asleep because I had given him very strong ale at dinner in the hope he would fall asleep before he could insist on being intimate.

But I could not sleep: I lay awake all night, full of joy and gladness about the bliss of heaven.

In the morning, I knew it was not the Lord's intention that I be quiet about my visions. As a woman I was not allowed to preach, as was declared by St Paul. But I could still tell of my experiences of Christ and heaven using conversation and good words, without going into any pulpit.

I was nervous, the first time I stood in the street and spoke about my visions. I stood on Wingate, between the new Guildhall and the River Ouse, and beckoned people to gather round me, for I had great tidings to tell. At first, only a few old women stopped to listen, but as I told of how Jesus visited me and blessed me, and how I had heard the music of heaven, a small crowd gathered.

This was most gratifying and I enjoyed myself, describing how handsome Jesus was, and how sweet his conversation. When I had finished, a woman pushed a coin into my hand and asked me to pray for her.

But not everyone was kind. 'Why do you talk so of the joy that is in heaven?' asked a rough young man, who had only joined the crowd at the end of my talk. 'You haven't been there any more than we have.'

This provoked much laughter and the rest of the crowd wandered off without giving me any coins or thanking me for my words.

Meanwhile, my husband was losing money like a tree loses leaves in the gales of autumn. He told me of his debts, and I was so alarmed that I set up as an alewife, even though I was expecting our fifth child very soon. The neighbours thought I was trying to earn money out of greed, for I did not tell them of John's debts. At first, it was a great success, and I do believe I was one of the greatest brewers in town. But after four years, my ale would no longer froth and every batch I made was bad. A rumour spread around Lynn that God was punishing me for my lies.

Then, at last, something good happened. Master Hugh died suddenly and a new priest came to St Margaret's by name of Robert Spryngolde. The first time I went to confession with him, I started at the beginning of my life, confessing my sins from childhood up until the very day we were both standing in. And Master Spryngolde listened patiently and was most kind. But it wasn't enough, because there was still the unconfessed sin stuck inside me.

So I made another visit to Master Spryngolde later that same day, and told him I had a very difficult sin to confess. He waited for me to say it and didn't cough or fidget as Master Hugh used to do. At last I was able to tell him of my stuck-inside sin: that of self-love, by rubbing my most private parts. I trembled as I spoke, and wondered if for such a severe sin he would tell me that I should be dealt with by the Bishop. Instead, he asked me quickly if I truly repented, and I said I did, and he told me to fast for a week, eating no meat or eggs, and that I would be absolved.

In truth, I was most disappointed. This sin had been troubling me for over ten years, so I fasted for two weeks to make sure, and abstained from milk and cheese as well as meat and eggs, as if it was Lenten time.

JULIAN

Simon returned to Norwich when I was fifteen. I met him in the street when I was walking with my mother. He was much changed but I knew him immediately.

My mother asked him questions about his journey, his family, his health. She told him he looked well. All the while our eyes were on each other's faces, something passing between us like lightning flashes. All thoughts of convents and tending a *hortus conclusus* were driven from my mind. My mother glanced at me and guessed what was between us.

Simon's father called at our house the next day. He spoke to my mother privately, and I fled to the garden, shredding several rose blooms while I waited to hear what was said.

My mother came outside and tutted at the damage. She took my hands in hers and told me that a marriage had been agreed, and that there would be wedding notice placed on the door of the Church of St Julian. I wept and hugged her, and then laughed to myself all day.

Later, my mother smiled and made a joke about 'reading lessons'.

Our wedding day was a day of such happiness it was as though sunlight flowed in our veins. We exchanged our vows and rings at the church door, before entering for the nuptial mass. Afterwards, my mother's cousin placed her baby in my arms and Simon's brother put a gold florin in my shoe; in this way, we were wished fertility and prosperity. A minstrel accompanied us to my mother's house where we feasted with friends and family.

That night I lay with my husband in naked honesty, eager to show my love, and there was much pleasure given and received all through the night.

MARGERY

It was around the time of the birth of my eighth child that my weeping began. Suddenly I found that I could not bear to think of Our Lord's Passion and suffering without weeping so loudly and copiously that people were astounded. Some people said I was putting it on, trying to cause trouble and get attention.

I begged Christ to forgive them. My husband begged me to dry my tears.

My father visited, saying he was hearing tales about me and it was causing him and my mother great distress. But I had no answer for him, for I could not stop the tears.

Street preachers asked me to move away from them because people could not hear their words over my sobbing, and some priests asked me to leave the church for the same reason, though not Master Robert. I asked God if he would make my sobbing quieter, for I would have rather wept softly and privately if it had been in my power; but God said my weeping did much good.

At this time, I was very strict in my habits. I was sometimes shriven two or three times a day, because I was so fearful of being kept from heaven if I were to be knocked down by a horse, or ate a bad pie, or died in some other sudden way. I would not want any unshriven sins to keep me from heaven even for a moment. I often rose at three o'clock, before it was light, and went to church where I knelt in prayer until midday and my knees were red as apples.

Robert Spryngolde said I must be a most holy and blessed woman indeed to give so much of my time to thoughts of Jesus and heaven. However, even Master Robert wondered about the cause of my weeping, and concocted a secret plan. He invited me to a different chapel, one that was little used, and then he left me at my prayers, saying he had to visit someone who was ill. But in fact he hid outside, and he heard me weeping and sorrowing when I thought I was alone. In this way he knew that my weeping was a gift from God and not pretence.

Yet still I was sometimes greatly depressed because I was so full of dread that my visions and my weeping were delusions, sent from the devil who is the father of all lies.

I consulted with many priests and friars, as well as with hermits and anchorites and other wise souls, as to whether my visions were true and holy, and while most gave me reassurance, still I was afraid.

I continued to speak about my visions in town and on some days many people gathered to hear my words. Yet others continued to laugh at me and insult my person. One man said, 'Woman, give up this life that you lead, and go and spin and card wool, as other women do, and do not suffer so much shame and unhappiness.'

But I answered that I suffered nothing in comparison to what Christ had suffered, and was well pleased with this reply.

JULIAN

Soon after the wedding I was with child, and when she was born we called her Elizabeth after my dead sister. She was a fine, black-curled creature with her father's blue eyes and my own long limbs. Like all new parents, we thought our child the most splendid ever to be born.

The pestilence that came then was swifter than the first. A person hardly knew they were ill before they were dead.

Simon left me first. One morning he could not get out of bed. I rushed out to buy a pinch of saffron, which had been much discussed lately as a cure. I brewed the yellow-orange threads with warm water, letting them steep for half an hour, and made him drink it down. But then he developed a headache and his throat was sore. Soon the fever took over and he was too weak to sit up. He sweated and complained of chills. I made another saffron brew and cradled his head in my lap, dripping the bright liquid on to his tongue. But I knew by then, and sent for Master Walter.

He did not come in time. Simon died in my arms, clawing at the air, without the priest's oil or the chance to confess. His last words were 'Love God'. Or were they, 'For the love of God'?

My heart grew as icy as his brow. I thought that nothing worse could ever befall me.

The next day Elizabeth's nurse came crying into my room, saying that the baby wouldn't suckle and her head was lolling.

I scooped Elizabeth into my arms. I prayed and prayed and prayed and prayed and prayed and prayed and prayed and prayed and prayed and prayed and prayed.

Within hours I was both a widow and childless. I sank to my knees and my own mother held me as I gasped out my pain in sobs and retching.

I thought I was falling into a black and bottomless pit. I begged God to deliver me from this life, for I no longer wanted it.

MARGERY

As well as seeing visions of Our Lord and hearing the music of heaven, I have been privileged to hear the Holy Ghost.

'What's that noise?' I asked my husband one evening when we were sitting together after our evening meal.

'The dog,' he muttered. 'That bitch thinks every leaf that falls to the ground is a thief or murderer. If she doesn't give it a rest, I'll tell Cook to put her in the pot.'

At this, one of my youngest daughters began to cry. 'I won't let Cook put her in a pot,' she wept. 'I'm not eating Dyamant!'

'Oh, hush your tears.' My husband gave her a quick smack. 'You cry almost as much as your mother.'

All the while that my good family were exchanging these words, I heard a noise in my ear as loud as the sound of air rushing through a pair of bellows, and I knew it was the sound of the Holy Ghost moving around me.

JULIAN

After the death of my husband and child, my mother and I wept together. I thought of Simon and Elizabeth, and she thought of my father and William and Bethy. I understood then that they had never left her thoughts and never would. Grief marks a person, changing them for ever, like a tree struck by lightning. The tree may keep growing, but never in the same way.

I thought long about the pestilence. Many people spoke of it as a punishment, but for what? What had we done that warranted such anger, such rage, such cruelty? Were all the dead guilty? The Church says we are all born into sin, but I struggled to understand why a baby should be so harshly punished.

I was so angry that I almost turned from God. I sorrow to think of that now. I blamed him for my loss, yet all the time he was there, comforting me though I could not see him. I prayed, but at first my ears were so stuffed with sorrow that I could hardly hear him. Master Walter visited and tried to comfort me, but he was a busy man with many dying people to visit. The pestilence had not touched our house alone.

For ten years I lived in grief with my mother. Suitors came, but I refused to marry again. I could think of nothing but my lost loves.

My solitude grew round me like a rind. I prayed that God would send me a sickness in which I would have every kind of suffering in body and spirit. I wanted to suffer as my loved ones had suffered; I wanted to feel what they had felt; I did not want them to leave me behind.

I prayed before the crucifix in church. I said to the Lord, 'Hurt me.'

Then, when I was thirty, God granted me my desire.

He sent me a fever.

MARGERY

One time I met a monk who seemed to despise me. 'I hear it said that God speaks to you,' he hissed at me, his hand on my sleeve. 'I wish to know if I am to be saved or not, and in what sins I have most displeased God. And I will not believe that God speaks to you unless you can tell me what my sins are.'

I shook off his hand, and went to mass. When it was over I prayed to Our Lord Jesus Christ and asked him what I should say to this man.

'Beloved daughter, say in the name of Jesus that his sins are lechery, despair and the keeping of worldly goods.'

I quailed at the thought of repeating such things to that monk, his eye was so flinty upon me.

But Jesus said, 'Do not be afraid, but speak boldly in my name, for these are not lies.'

Then I asked Jesus if the monk would be saved, and he said he would, if he gave up his sins and was shriven of them.

So I went to the monk again, and when he saw me he demanded, 'Margery, tell me my sins.'

I hesitated and said, 'I beg you, sir, do not ask me to name them. Just confess them and do not commit them again, and you will be saved.'

But he said, 'I won't believe that God speaks to you unless you tell me what my sins are.'

So I told him, 'You have sinned in lechery, despair and the keeping of worldly goods.'

He stood very still, his hands frozen at his sides. 'Have I sinned with wives or with single women?'

The answer sprang into my mind, as if Jesus was still speaking with me in my soul. 'Sir, with wives,' I said.

He swallowed. 'But I will be saved?'

'Yes, if you are shriven and give up those sins. God will give you grace because he loves me, his precious daughter, and because I have asked it of him.'

Then he thanked me and took me into a beautiful room where he gave me a great dinner, and afterwards he gave me gold to pray for him.

JULIAN

My fever was not the pestilence, but some kind of sweating sickness. My mother burnt angelica, chamomile and coriander seeds to purify the air, and she propped my failing body beside the fire to drive out its heat. The sweat poured out of me, soaking cloth after cloth, as if I was made only of water.

She tipped rosehip tea into my foul-smelling mouth and placed sage and rosemary under my pillow. But I grew more ill, sweating and shivering and calling out for her, though she was always by my side.

Master Walter came and I gave my confession and received the Eucharist. Soon I approached oblivion. The room grew dark as my sight began to fail. I could no longer move the lower part of my body and my limbs were weak as softened wax. My mother closed my eyelids, murmuring of her love for me, her only remaining child.

I felt her love enclose me, like a caress, and I was not afraid. I thought, so this is death!

But when the priest held up the crucifix, somehow I could see it there in front of me, as if my eyes were open and my sight restored, yet I saw it only with the eye of my understanding.

It was then that I saw globules of blood trickle down from Christ's crown of thorns, so fresh and plenteous I thought it would soak the sheets, as it did when I was in childbed. This was my first *shewing*. And as I lay there, insensible to my own body, I had another fourteen *shewings*.

Shewing Two: Still looking at Master Walter's crucifix, I saw Jesus' face change colour. I saw that dear face go ashen. There was dry blood on his temples and under his jaw. As he got nearer to death, his face went blue, then darker blue as the flesh mortified more completely. It was a sorrowful change and I saw his nose was shrivelled. I heard the words that Christ spoke: 'I thirst.' And I thought that the drying of Christ's flesh was the greatest agony.

The blessed body was drying for a long time, becoming distorted because of the nails and the heaviness of the head. Then a wind began to blow, that dried him and tormented him more than I can imagine. I saw such pains that everything I could say would be inadequate, for they were indescribable. He was dying in front of me, and I glimpsed the true of horror of his death.

I realised then that if I had truly understood his suffering, I would not have asked to share in it. I prayed to God then, full of repentance for my anger towards him who had given his only son.

Then a voice instructed me to look up, away from Christ's suffering, but I refused. I would not leave him, even though it might kill me to stay. Jesus spoke to me from the cross: 'Lo, how I love thee.' And I understood that this was true, and that he hadn't actually spoken these words, but had shown them to be true through his suffering.

Shewing Three: I saw God in an instant and understood that he was all things.

I understood that faith was not something to be demanded, but must be sought, and that no matter how close to God we felt, we would always want to be closer, and that this was how it should be. Faith was striving, not being at ease.

Then my consciousness was taken down to the seabed, where I saw hills and valleys covered with sand and seaweed, and I understood that even if a man or woman were under the wide waters, they would be able to see God if they sought him.

Shewing Four: I saw blood flow from Jesus' wounds, but then vanish as if there had never been any blood at all.

Shewing Five: God showed me that his Passion defeats the devil.

Shewing Six: God thanked me for my suffering and showed me the bliss of heaven.

Shewing Seven: God gave me alternating experiences of sorrow and joy. And I saw that neither of these matter, for we live on earth only a short time, and our lives are shaken by sorrow like a cloth in the wind, but we should take it lightly, for we are in heaven with God a long time after.

Shewing Eight: I saw that Christ shared in the pain felt by all creatures.

Shewing Nine: Jesus Christ affirmed his pleasure in suffering for my sake. And I thought how Christ is like a mother, and loves us like a mother. Didn't he labour in agony on the cross that we might have life?

Shewing Ten: Christ directed my gaze into his wound, where the soldier had thrust his spear. Peering between his ribs I saw his heart, and it was riven in two. I could see into the chambers of that great heart, and within it I saw the Kingdom of Heaven, like a large and glittering city, with room for all of mankind who shall be saved.

Shewing Eleven: Jesus asked if I would like to see his blessed mother, Our Lady Mary, and I answered, 'Yes, my good Lord, thank you.' I thought I would see her bodily presence on earth, but it was a spiritual vision, and she was noble and glorious.

Shewing Twelve: God revealed himself in glory.

Shewing Thirteen: God affirmed that, despite sin and suffering, all shall be well. He told me that this will be by means of a 'Great Deed' to be performed at the end of the world, though he did not tell me the nature of this deed.

Then I requested to know how it would be with a certain person I loved. And in this request I stood in my own path, for I was not answered immediately. But I heard the voice, as if from a friendly man, saying in my head, 'Take these *shewings* generally, and consider the kindness of your Lord as he gives them to you.'

Then I knew it was not my place to ask God specific questions, nor to rejoice over any special thing or be distressed by any particular thing; instead I should keep in mind that all shall be well, as God had said.

Shewing Fourteen: God told me how much prayer pleases him.

Shewing Fifteen: God promised I would be rewarded for my suffering.

These fifteen visions lasted many hours and during them many words were spoken in my mind. I called out 'Benedicite Dominus!' and also 'Today is my Doomsday' because I thought I was dying, and sometimes I laughed with joy. I wanted to tell my mother not to worry, that the only pain I felt was the pain of Christ, but I could not speak with any other words than the ones just described.

Whilst I had been experiencing these *shewings* the suffering of my own sickness had abated, but as soon as I awoke my sickness returned, first in my head, which was full of noise, and then in my whole body which felt dry and barren.

I went to sleep but I suffered terrible dreams. The devil was at my throat, thrusting his face into mine. It was like a young man's face, but extraordinarily long and thin, and it was as red as newly fired tiles. Rust-red locks hung over his temples and he grinned at me, showing his pointy teeth. His paws gripped my throat and tried to strangle me, but he could not. I trusted to God I would be protected by his mercy. When I woke up, I was barely alive.

My mother bathed my face and tended to me, but I smelt smoke and a great heat coming from the door. There was a foul stench and I cried out, 'Benedicite domine! Everything is on fire!' I thought we were all going to burn to death.

'There's no fire, daughter,' my mother said. 'Calm yourself.'

I knew that the devil had come to torment me, so I directed my thoughts to those *shewings* the Lord had given me by way of comfort, and immediately the terrors of my mind fled and I was brought to a great state of rest and peace.

Then my mother was on her knees, praising the Lord that I was alive, but I was too weak to lift my head or drink more than a little water boiled with lemon balm.

MARGERY

There were times when I had little money and could not give to the poor or the church as I would have liked. But Jesus told me that he knew every thought of my heart, and that if I did have money, he knew I would found many abbeys for his love, and that if I could, I would pay for many priests who might sing and read night and day to serve him.

So he said, 'Therefore, daughter, you shall have the same reward in heaven for these good wills and desires, as if you had done them indeed.'

I told my friend and neighbour Agnes what he had said. She smiled slightly and patted my arm. 'Sometimes, Margery, when we want to see something, it can seem to appear before our very eyes.'

I didn't know what she was talking about, but her baby had recently died so I thought perhaps she was still grief-mad.

JULIAN

When I awoke again, it was the next day and the streets were full of life. And it was then that I received my final *shewing*:

Shewing Sixteen: God showed me Jesus in my soul and assured me that my *shewings* came from him. It is difficult to express how God spoke to me, how he gave me understanding. He didn't use words like those we use among ourselves, but in my soul I heard him say, 'Know well now that what you saw was no delirium; accept and believe it, and comfort yourself with it, and you shall not be overcome.'

It seemed to me that the last *shewing* was the most important, but I could not fully understand its meaning. It was as God told Isaiah: *For my thoughts are not your thoughts, neither are your ways my ways.*

I had no further *shewings*, and from that time on, I thought of my life in two parts – before the *shewings* and after.

With my mother's tender care, I recovered from my illness, but my spirits were low. I had been with Christ and he had said, 'Lo, how I love thee,' but now we were apart.

I asked my mother if she had seen Jesus' blood flowing from his head. She flashed me a look full of fear, and gripped my wrist and said, 'No, daughter.' And I never spoke of what I had seen again.

Soon after this, Master Walter died, and we had a new priest, Master Thomas. He was beakish and spoke more often of hell and damnation. I knew not to confide in him what I had seen, no matter that I was sure my *shewings* had come from God.

But whilst I did not speak of my *shewings*, I thought of them constantly. I was so afraid of forgetting them that as soon as I was well enough, I busied myself with writing them down. I wrote hurriedly when my mother was out of the house, for she neither liked me to write, nor would she have liked what I was writing about.

I wrote down what I had seen and what I had heard, yet there was so much more to these *shewings*. There was *understanding* and I knew I did not have that yet. I needed time and space to think.

I no longer thought of becoming a nun, as I had before my marriage, because now I knew that the life of a nun was busy, every hour taken up with praying, singing, cleaning, husbandry, wine-making, sewing, record-keeping or teaching the novices.

It seemed the only way I would have the time I needed to reflect on my *shewings* was to become a recluse. I knew about people who had given up their possessions and lived in one room, or even in a damp cave, and did nothing but pray. Indeed, my mother and I had visited a hermit together some years before, at Bawburgh, a few miles to the west of the city. He had his own chapel and he blessed pilgrims who passed on their way to Norwich, sprinkling them with hyssop and holy water. My mother gave him some coins and he blessed us too and prayed for our souls. He had a saintly air and a quietness to his expression, as if time passed more slowly for him. He had a gentle way of moving too, that I had always imagined of St Francis, who could tame the birds from the trees and coax the fox from its hole.

At the time I had been struck by the simplicity of his way of life, although I had no thought of living like this myself. But now, such a thought took me over. Hermits were free to wander as they pleased, begging for alms in exchange for prayers. I spoke to Master Thomas about it, but he said that hermits were usually men, because it was not safe for women to wander alone. Women who wanted a secluded life became anchoresses, taking a vow of anchorage and remaining solely in one place, such as in a cell attached to a church.

An anchoress. I had heard of such women, of course, and had read about them in Walter Hilton's *The Scale of Perfection*, but I had not truly thought about the meaning of the word 'anchoress' before. To reside in one place and devote my thoughts to God; to be an anchor for God. To be anchored to God.

But I could not be an anchoress — not while my mother was alive. To remove myself from her would have been a terrible cruelty, for we were each other's only living kin.

So we lived together, two widows, for another dozen years. My mother's death came suddenly, but it was gentle, thank God in his mercy. One morning, she was not up before me. That was so unusual that I went to her chamber. She was lying under the coverlet, her hands clasped above it. She opened her eyes when I approached, but did not turn her head.

'My daughter, is that you?' she called.

'Yes, Mother.' I sat on the chair at her bedside and stroked her hands. I felt the long bones of her fingers through skin as delicate as that on boiled milk. Her night cap had come loose and her long grey hair was spread out on the pillow, rough as a pony's mane.

'Pray for me, daughter. I will soon be with Our Lord.'

I rang for the maid and told her to fetch the priest. Then I got to my knees.

> *Ave Maria, gratia plena, Dominus tecum.*
> *Benedicta tu in mulieribus, et benedictus fructus ventris tui, Iesus.*
> *Sancta Maria, Mater Dei, ora pro nobis peccatoribus, nunc,*
> *et in hora mortis nostrae.*
> *Amen.*

MARGERY

There were some months when I was very untroubled of spirit. I fasted a great deal and enjoyed my conversations with Jesus, and had little interest in worldly joys. I wore my hair shirt and was very full of the love of God. I did not notice I was smitten with the sin of vainglory.

But God noticed and he sent me a temptation, laying a snare where he knew I was frail.

I had thought that all the lust had long been quenched out of me by my husband, and although we continued to lie together it had become horrible to me.

But then it happened that a man whom I liked approached me before evensong on St Margaret's Eve. He smiled at me and fell into stride beside me. As we walked along, remarking on the mild evening, he took my hand in his and began caressing my fingers. Then he brought them to his lips. 'Margery,' he murmured. And he said he would like to sleep with me and enjoy the lust he felt for my body.

He said my name tenderly, as my husband used to when we were first married, and I felt my body warm in response.

I did not say anything in reply to this man, but went directly into church. I could hardly listen to evensong or even say my paternoster or think any good thoughts because I was thinking about what he had said. Then the devil put it into my mind that God had forsaken me, for why else would I be thinking all these thoughts, instead of praying and thinking about God's love?

So when evensong was over I went over to the man as he was leaving and said that he could have his will. But he looked at me as if he had never said any of those words that I had heard him say before and walked away from me.

I was most vexed and troubled all the night. In truth, I very much wanted to sin with this man.

JULIAN

Master Thomas gave my mother her final sacraments, and soon she was in the Lord's embrace. She died peacefully and shriven, and I was free to follow God's path.

Two weeks after my mother's burial, I visited Master Thomas to tell him what I had decided. He raised an eyebrow, but didn't question my resolve. He said that because I was not part of a religious order, I would need to have a meeting with the Bishop of Norwich, for I must prove that I was a suitable person for anchorage, and that my mind and body were prepared for isolation and confinement.

'The church is not interested in unstable persons,' he said. 'An anchorage is not a place of respite from the terrors of one's own mind.'

I was interviewed by Henry le Despenser, Bishop of Norwich, also called the Fighting Bishop for his manner of quelling the peasants when they rioted and plundered our city a few years ago. I was fearful of meeting him but he was genial enough and did not seem much interested in either my mind or my spiritual journey. Instead, he asked me about my wealth: an anchoress must pay her way. I had inherited much of my mother's estate as well as having my dower after Simon's death, so could reassure him on that point. I made over all my property and money to the church, apart from a stipend which would cover my food and other expenses, and also a maid's wages. Then the Bishop gave me his blessing and a guide for anchoresses, the *Ancrene Wisse*.

MARGERY

The next day I went to see the man who had kissed my fingers, and asked again if he would have me. He glared at me and said not for all the wealth in this world; he said he would rather be chopped up small as meat for the pot.

I went away, full of shame and confusion. I thought about all the grace that God had given me and how I'd been sure I would never again be tempted, but how, as soon as I was flattered by a man, I had been willing to commit adultery.

I thought myself in hell then, so great was my sorrow. I deserved no mercy, so wilful was my choice to sin. I went immediately to be shriven, and was shriven many times and often, and did all the penance Master Robert enjoined me to do.

In church I looked at the paintings of adulterers suffering in hell, and thought how easily I was nearly one myself. Just remembering sent me to confession again, for I could not get enough of being shriven of my sins.

JULIAN

There is a ceremony to become an anchoress. A nun is a bride of Christ and so has a nuptial mass, but becoming an anchorite is a death.

I had to die to the world.

I bade farewell to my friends and asked them not to attend the ceremony or visit me in my cell. I dressed in black and walked alone to church, my hands trembling a little. I asked God to give me courage and serenity. I was just a woman, but he gave me strength.

I stood before the Bishop and Master Thomas. Other priests and men of the church stood to the side, witnesses to the ceremony and no doubt curious – it was not every day that a church acquired a recluse.

My voice was quiet but calm as I made my vows of poverty, chastity and stability of abode.

I gave up my name.

For the second time in my life, I was given last rites and felt the cool oil slip across my forehead.

Then I lay on the floor and a black cloak was placed over me.

A requiem mass was sung, the priests' voices lifting in sorrowful melody. If I hadn't been lying down, I would have swooned.

> *Requiem aeternam dona eis, Domine,*
> *et lux perpetua luceat eis.*

For two hours I lay on the cold stone flags, covered by my black cloak. I listened to the voices rise and fall.

Te decet hymnus, Deus, in Sion,
et tibi reddetur votum in Jerusalem:
exaudi orationem meam,
ad te omnis caro veniet.
Requiem æternam dona eis, Domine:
et lux perpetua luceat eis.

I smelt the incense as the Bishop swung the thurible over me. Then he touched me on the shoulder and I got to my feet.

The Bishop and the priests followed me into the church-yard singing '*In paradisum deducant te angeli*', the notes slow and solemn, each one a step into the next life.

My cell was on the north side of the church. I approached it, a sudden wind chilling me as I waited for the Bishop's words that were the signal for me to enter:

If she wishes to go in, allow her to go in.

The choir sang, 'Be of good courage, thy desire from God is at hand.'

And I stepped inside.

The floor of the cell was bare earth, with fresh reeds scattered over it and violets for a sweet scent.

I stood in my cell and the Bishop and Master Thomas scattered earth on my shoulders, to remind me that I was come from the earth and would return to the earth.

Then they stepped out of my cell and two workmen stepped forward. In silence, they bricked up the door.

I knelt on the floor, dazed and fearful.

I wanted my mind to be driven deep into God like a nail.

MARGERY

It was just before Christmas Day, when I was kneeling in church and begging for forgiveness from the Lord, when Jesus came to me again. He ravished my soul and spoke these words in my mind:

'Daughter, why are you weeping so sorely? I have come to you, Jesus Christ who died on the cross, suffering bitter pains for you. And I, the same God, forgive your sins. And you shall never go to hell or even to purgatory, but when you pass out of this world you shall be in heaven in the twinkling of an eye.'

Then he said, 'And daughter, leave off wearing your hair shirt.'

At this I was most surprised but also relieved, for my back and chest were covered in welts and scabs.

He also said, 'Go to the anchorite at the Preaching Friars, and tell him my confidences and counsels which I reveal to you, and do as he tells you, for I will speak through him to you.'

Well, this I did, and the anchorite, with much weeping, thanked God and said, 'Truly daughter, you are sucking at Christ's breast.'

At this I shuddered. I knew the anchorite meant well, but it reminded me of my babies, their mouths always grasping at me, sucking me dry.

I mentioned to my neighbour, Agnes, that Jesus had spoken to me again and she said, 'I tell you as a friend, Margery, to stop your nonsense. Nobody believes it and you are doing yourself no good. It doesn't behove you to tell these lies. People will shun you and your husband too. Then see how well his trade goes.'

These words stung like a hornet, and I was greatly saddened. But then I realised that this was part of my trial on earth, as ordained by God, and that many saints and holy women, including Bridget of Sweden, had been called liars by foolish people who knew no better and who were not visited by Jesus.

JULIAN

Those early days, weeks, months, years of being in my cell – I am glad I will not live through them again. Though I knew that God would send me trials and tribulations, I did not predict the form that these would take.

I had thought I was ready for the life of an anchoress. I had wanted to prolong each moment of my life, to get closer to experiencing time as God experiences it: not the instantly dissolving moment, but something larger and more encompassing. A stillness that doesn't pass as soon as you think yourself into it.

I'd thought I would live as slowly as moss in my stone cell. I'd thought I would step out of my life as soon as I stepped into the cell. But I was still me. Nothing had changed. I was myself, with all my usual racing thoughts and yearnings and memories and foolishness.

Nothing can prepare you for spending the rest of your life in a single room. Never to be touched by another human being. Never to run. Never to feel the rain on your face. Never to walk in the garden and see flowers unfolding their colours and scents.

I had died to the world, died to my old life, but I was not dead.

Sara brought me food and firewood, but in those early days we did not know each other. She was careful to follow Master Thomas' orders not to distract me with what he called 'women's chatter'. She treated me like a holy saint, whispering, 'Mother Julian, I have your supper.' I could almost hear her curtseying on the other side of the curtain.

How I yearned for women's chatter.

As well as loneliness, idleness was to be my trial. I was unused to having so little to do or to look at, and what things I could do, I did not want to do. The *Ancrene Wisse* instructs anchoresses to pray and meditate every day, and to recite psalms from the Office of the Dead, but if they cannot bring their mind to these things they should sew vestments for the church. Otherwise they should simply be silent.

Master Thomas came to take my confession and give me the sacrament, but I hardly knew what he said to me or I to him. I was too ashamed to admit the truth. That I was unhappy and afraid in my cell. That I did not want to pray. Or recite psalms. Or meditate. Or sew.

Nor did I want to think about my *shewings*. I had brought my papers with me, on which I had written down what I had seen. I re-read my words, as I had done many times before. But it was as if they had eroded: they seemed provisional, mere attempts at thought, a scattering of words which suggested little of those vivid experiences when I lay in my bed and looked upon the body of Christ.

I spent these early months in a state of nothingness and weeping. Months of inactivity, nothing achieved, time leaching away. I felt unable to move, to act, to think. Everything seemed both pointless and overwhelming.

Stone walls. Stone walls. Stone walls. Stone walls. Stone walls. Stone walls. Stone walls. Stone walls. Stone walls.

Stone walls.

God have mercy on me.

Stone walls.

God have mercy.

Stone walls.

God.

Stone walls.

MARGERY

I continued speaking to the people of Lynn about my conversations with Jesus, but Agnes was proved right that many townsfolk did not like it. People avoided me in the street, crossing even where there was filth in the gutter.

My husband complained that men made jokes at my expense within his hearing, and that he would not be elected an alderman if I did not stop my lies.

But not everyone was angry with me. Some people gave me money to pray for them. Some people thought I was a prophetess and asked me questions about whether a person who was ill would get better. I consulted with God in my mind and he gave me the answer, yea or nay, and later it would always prove to be true.

Some people thought I was a healer. Once I was in the Church of St Margaret, saying my devotions, when

I perceived a man kneeling and wringing his hands. I asked him what was troubling him and he said things were very difficult for him, because his wife had just had a baby and was out of her mind.

'She doesn't know me or any of her neighbours. She roars and cries, so that she scares people. She hits out and bites, so she's manacled on her wrists.'

I asked the man if he would like me to go with him and see her and he said, 'Yes, lady, for God's love.'

And as soon as that sick woman who had lost her reason saw me, she spoke most seriously and kindly, and said I was most welcome to her. 'For you are,' she said, 'a very good woman, and I behold many fair angels round about you, and therefore, I pray you, don't leave me, for I am greatly comforted by you.'

But when other people came, she cried and gaped as if she would have eaten them, and said that she saw many devils around them. She was taken to a room at the furthest end of town, so that people should not hear her crying.

I went to her each day, once or twice at least, and while I was with her she was meek enough, chatting willingly without any crying or roaring. And I prayed every day that God should, if it was his will, restore her to her wits again. And he answered in my soul that she would get on very well, as I had after the birth of my own child, and soon she was well enough to be brought to church and purified as other women are, blessed may God be. Those who heard about it thought it a very great miracle – worship and praise be to Our Lord for his high mercy and goodness, who ever helps at times of need.

JULIAN

The nights were hardest. Night asks many questions that day turns her face from.

I was often sleepless, unpraying, just waiting for dawn and the distractions of visitors, meals, bells.

I remembered Master Thomas' words: *An anchorage is not a place of respite from the terrors of one's own mind.* Now I was alone with my terrors. I dwelt on my sins. I fretted that Simon had died unshriven. My mind showed my husband in Eternal Torment and would not let me rest.

I had wanted to be alone with God but he seemed far away. I had thought a cell would be a spiritual retreat, but it was nothing more than an earth-floored shack, full of woodlice and earwigs. I felt disgust for my cell. Its darkness. Its dankness. For the creeping, scuttling things that shared it with me. For my own foul mortal flesh. I ate and drank and used my pot; I bit off my fingernails when they grew long; I slept and woke and I breathed in and out all day long. There was nothing spiritual about me. I tried to pray but could hardly begin. What must all our beseeching prayers sound like to God, I wondered – all our pleas and petty bargains? Like nothing more than the twitter of birds.

Every day I struggled to get up. The air in my cell tasted bitter. I wanted to scream, but held my tongue for fear of being overheard.

Instead of thinking about my *shewings*, my mind kept running back to the past, like water flowing downhill.

I remembered being a child, especially that winter when the first pestilence came. I remembered something I had forgotten for many years: seeing, from the window, a body lying on the ground. It was swollen and rotting, with no shape or form. It was a person who had become one with the stinking mire.

I remembered my nurse Joan forcing me to clear my plate, even though all that remained was gristle. I remember the feel of the hard lumps pushing down my throat.

I remembered my father's loud voice, the way he raised his voice and hands to my mother. I remember the looks of hate my brother William threw him.

I remembered the stench of my sister Bethy as a baby, and how her wailing woke the household for many nights when her first tooth pierced her gum.

And I remembered when they died, how their bodies were dragged into the street, and a white cross was chalked on our door.

I remembered Simon and my own baby, how their bodies were taken from the house, and how there was no grave for me to visit.

The only respite from these memories was sleep, but soon after I entered my cell I began to dream of the life I had lost, as a blind man still dreams in pictures.

I dreamt of Simon – chipped tooth, sunlit hair, his limp which was always worse when the weather was cold or damp.

I dreamt of Simon touching me.

I dreamt of Simon kissing me.

I dreamt of Simon talking to me, saying something I couldn't quite hear.

As I leant towards him, I woke up. Back in my small dark cell.

MARGERY

Jesus commanded me to stop praying so much, saying that even if I said a thousand paternosters every day, it would please him more if I was silent and allowed him to speak.

But I liked praying, because it gave me a reason to be at church and not at home. I lay on a stone bench in church, waiting for him to speak. It was dull and there was no one else in church except the verger, who was dusting the censer and giving me odd looks. So I said in my mind, 'Jesus, what shall I think about?'

And he replied, 'Daughter, think of my mother.'

And in my contemplation suddenly I saw St Anne, Our Lady's mother. She was great with child and I was her maid. Soon Our Lady was born, and I looked after her until she was twelve years old, giving her food and drink, and dressing her in nice white clothes. And I said to her, 'My Lady, you shall be the Mother of God!'

I thought she would faint or fall to her knees in thanks, or at least kiss me. But instead she replied, cool as a fresh herring, 'I wish that I were worthy enough to even be the handmaiden of a woman that should conceive the Son of God.'

'*You* shall be that woman!' I insisted, but she was too modest to be troubled by my words. So then I said, 'Promise me that if that grace does befall you, you will let me continue to be of service to you,' and the blessed child agreed.

The child went away and then returned – and all this time I was still in my contemplation – and she said to me, 'Now I have become the Mother of God.'

And then I fell to my knees, and with great weeping said, 'I am not worthy, my Lady, to do you service.'

And she answered, 'Daughter, I am well pleased with your service.'

Together we visited her cousin, Elizabeth, and I dandled little John the Baptist on my knee, and Elizabeth said to me, 'Daughter, it seems to me you do your duty very well.'

And then I found myself travelling with the Virgin Mother to Bethlehem. I was trying to find a room for her to have her baby and I spoke to many people, but they all shrugged and said it was the census so everywhere was busy. Indeed, it was quite the busiest town I had ever visited.

Then an innkeeper, quite handsome except for his large belly, winked at me and said that although he had no rooms free, he had a stable. At first I was insulted, but he took me round the back and I saw that, with a little work, I could make it quite comfortable. So I asked for water and a brush, and I scrubbed it as well as I could. The innkeeper came and said I had done well and gave me some clean straw and a piece of linen. I lay the linen on the straw and tried the bed and it was almost as comfortable as my own. So I fetched Mary and led her into the stable, and then I helped her with the birth.

Jesus was a fine, fat baby and as I swaddled him I wept tears at the thought of the painful death that was reserved for him. I said to him, 'Lord, I shall treat you gently; I will not bind you tightly. I pray you not to be displeased with me.'

Then I told Mary she must truly be a holy woman not to have cried out in labour. Not like me, who screamed and shouted and cursed, for the pain was really very bad with all my babies.

JULIAN

I dreamt of things I missed — the feel of my mother's best silk, the taste of gold-white cream, fresh from the dairy, watching the swans preening themselves on the river. And I dreamt of things I didn't miss — the sound of the death carts in the street, seeing a crow stoned to death by boys, and the time I was whipped by my father for sloth.

But I didn't dream of Elizabeth. If I wanted to remember my baby (oh, my child!), her skin, her black curls, her fingers clenched round mine, if I wanted to remember, I had to do it myself. I had to wade through all the pain and grief, force myself through it, to find the shining pictures of her that my mind had locked away. Her small, red mouth at my nipple, sucking desperately. The wodge of fat at her elbow, dimpled and kissable. Those joyful, kicking feet; those sweet gurgles; the scent of her skull, as clean and scented as meadowsweet.

I was her mother and I had let her die.

To say I wept would not be to convey the wracking sobs that convulsed my body.

And one day I thought, does God ever weep? Did he weep when his son was flayed and crucified? Did he even *look* as Jesus died? And if God could resurrect his own son, why not my daughter? What harm would that do?

But there were no answers to these questions.

The walls of my cell seemed very close. I walked around it, my sleeve brushing bed, desk, cupboard. I could take ten paces in one direction, turn and take six paces, turn and take eight paces, turn and take six paces.

Ten. Six. Eight. Six.

Ten. Six. Eight. Six.

Ten. Six. Eight. Six.

Ten. Six. Eight. Six.

Ten. Six. Eight. Six.

Ten. Six. Eight. Six.

MARGERY

In another vision I was at Christ's Passion, with Our
Lady and the disciples. I saw Christ on the cross, and I
wept as plenteously as if I was seeing him with my bodily
eyes. He had a nail through each wrist, and another that
went through both feet.

I saw his precious, tender body, all rent and torn with
scourges, and more full of holes than a dove-cote. Blood
flowed from every limb, and the wound in his precious
side was shedding out blood for my salvation.

I stood in the streets of Lynn and people flocked to hear
about my visions. As I spoke and remembered Jesus'
Passion, I could not keep myself from weeping, though
I should have been killed for it. I fell down and twisted
and turned my body on every side because the fire of
love burned so fervently in my soul, and called out
things, like 'Jesus, mercy!' and 'I die!'

I heard someone shout that I had drunk too much wine and
should go home to my husband. I called out to them that
I had drunk no wine, but only the sweet words of Jesus.

'And why wouldn't I cry?' I asked the people gathered
about me. 'For every day we see men and women who

are parted from their loved ones, and they also cry and roar and wring their hands as if they were out of their minds.'

The people nodded, for they had all seen such sorrowing with their own eyes.

'And if anyone advises them to leave off their weeping,' I continued, 'they would say that they could not, for they loved their departed one so much, and that they were so kind and gentle they will never forget them.'

One lady dabbed a handkerchief to her face at these words, and I knew she was thinking of a departed soul that she herself had loved and mourned. I fixed my eyes on her, as if addressing her directly. 'How much more you might weep if your dear departed was violently seized in front of your eyes, and wrongfully condemned to death, especially so shameful a death as our merciful Lord suffered for our sake. How would you bear it?'

Many people gave me coins that day, and asked me to pray for them. I took the money home and thought at first to give it to John, who was always complaining of our debts, but he was ill-tempered with me so I hid the money and did not tell him of my hoard.

JULIAN

Ten. Six. Eight. Six.

Ten. Six. Eight. Six.

I was wearing myself out to no purpose. I wondered if my mind was unravelling. What would that be like? All the threads come loose, waving in the wind. Perhaps I no longer wished to be ravelled.

MARGERY

Sometimes, when I saw a man with a wound, or a wounded beast, or saw a man beat a child, in my mind I saw Our Lord being beaten and wounded. And then I wept and roared, no matter whether I was in church or at the market.

I suffered much contempt and reproof for my weeping. It was so loud it astounded people, unless they had heard it before, and it made me very weak in my bodily strength. If people asked me what was wrong, I would cry out, 'The Passion of Christ slays me!'

Once, while I was standing outside St Margaret's at Easter, a fit of weeping came over me, and my husband said I was embarrassing him. A crowd grew around me and many people reproved me, but some comforted me and gave me their kerchiefs.

I begged people to listen to Jesus, for otherwise eternal damnation awaited them. The tears came strong, wetting my robe and every kerchief I was given, and my husband walked away, as if he did not know me.

Sometimes when I felt the urge to weep, I would try to hold it in, knowing people would get annoyed. Some said it was a wicked spirit tormenting me; others said it was an illness; some cursed me, wishing me at sea in a bottomless boat. Once, Agnes' husband Richard passed me when I was weeping, and he spat at the ground in front of my feet.

Because of this, I did all I could to suppress my weeping, but I would turn the colour of lead and it would seethe inside of me until it burst out. And the more I tried to keep it in, the louder I would weep.

JULIAN

With so little to look at, I listened: Sara, singing to herself. Dogs barking. The birds. In spring the cuckoo was persistent. In summer, my ears filled with the hum of insects. Swallows nested outside my cell, swooping and chattering. I blessed them, for they had plucked the thorns from Jesus' crown.

And always, always, there was the sound of the wind. Sometimes it brought rumours of snow from the east, sometimes the rivery scent of thaw.

One morning it was snowing and I put my hand out of my window. A few soft flakes landed on my palm and melted to form a pool. I brought it to my mouth and drank the world. As I did so, I thought of St Kevin. He extended his arm from his cave and in his upturned palm a blackbird made a nest and laid three blue eggs. Kevin kept his arm outstretched until the eggs hatched and three glossy-feathered young were ready for the wind to lift them away.

When Master Thomas came to hear my confession that day, he said that touching the snow was no sin. I wondered if I had confessed the wrong thing. It was not touching snow that I should have confessed, it was the feeling that led me to touch it. The feeling of despair.

Despair is the worst sin of all, because it comes between a person and God, blocking the light and causing torment to the soul. I had faced despair before, when my husband and baby died, but I did not know any path around it.

MARGERY

I had started standing near the Guildhall every Tuesday afternoon, so that anyone who wished to hear my latest vision would know where to find me. 'Hear me, good people of Lynn!' I called out. 'Listen to the story of Jesus' suffering!'

'Oh, it's Kempe's woman again,' I heard a man mutter. 'You were there, were you?' he called. 'At Jesus' birth *and* his death? You do get about.'

I made no reply, but continued with my story. 'I was there, and so was Our Lady, and we were both weeping to see the Lord on the cross. I knew the Lord wanted me to comfort his mother, so I said to her, "I pray you, Lady, you must cease from your sorrowing, for your son is dead and out of pain." And I saw the Lord's friends take his body from the cross and lay it before Our Lady on a marble stone. Our Lady bowed down to her son's body and kissed his mouth, and wept so plentifully over his blessed face that she washed away the blood with her tears.'

A few people gasped, which pleased me.

'Our Lady went homewards, so I went with her and made her a hot drink of gruel and spiced wine to comfort her, but Our Lady said, "Take it away, daughter. Give me no food but my own child."'

A woman who was listening with a baby in her arms bent her head and kissed the child then, as if she too wanted nothing but her child in her arms.

'A little later I was in a chapel with Our Lady, when Lord Jesus Christ appeared and said, "*Salve, sancta parens.*"'

At this point I heard a woman say to her friend, 'Margery Kempe is very learned, you know.'

I continued, 'And I heard Our Lady reply, "Are you my beloved son, Jesus?"

'"Yes, my blessed mother. I am your son, Jesus," he said. Then he took his mother in his arms and kissed her very sweetly.

'I saw Our Lady search all over Our Lord's body to see if there was any soreness or pain, but he said, "Dear Mother, my pain is all gone, and now I shall live for evermore."'

The crowd *ahh*ed at that, and there was a smattering of applause.

'I've not finished!' I told them. 'So then Jesus said he had to go and see Mary Magdalene. And Our Lady replied, "That is well done, son, for she has very great sorrow over your absence."'

An ugly, rude woman, whom I have never liked, called out, 'The Virgin Mary talks like a Lynn housewife!'

I glared at her, but she was looking around for approving looks from others.

'Well, soon after this,' I told them, 'I was with Mary Magdalene, mourning the Lord at his grave. And I saw him appear to Mary in the likeness of a gardener – yes, as scruffy as some of you standing here – and Jesus said, "Woman, why are you weeping?"'

'Mary Magdalene did not recognise him, and was all enflamed with the fire of love, replying, "Sir, if you have taken away my Lord, tell me, and I shall take him back again."'

'Then our merciful Lord, having pity and compassion on her, said' (and here I dropped my voice to a husky whisper), '"Mary". And with that word she knew him and fell down at his feet, saying, "Master", and went to kiss his feet. But he said to her, "Touch me not." Well, if he had spoken to me like that I'd never have been happy again. Then he said to go and tell his brethren that he had risen, and Mary went with great rejoicing.'

I had finished my vision, but people were still looking expectantly, so I added, 'And *that* was my vision of Jesus' death and resurrection.'

Again, a few people pressed coins into my hand, but I was surprised I did not get as much as in previous weeks. One woman came up to me and when I opened my hand she slapped it away and said, 'God will take his vengeance on you for your lies, Margery Kempe.'

JULIAN

At first I lived like a creature in its burrow. My desire was ashes.

The fact that Simon had died unshriven was like a wound I could not stop touching.

I tried to smother my thoughts with prayer, hardly thinking of the meaning of what I was saying to God. Every day I stood at my narrow cruciform window looking into the church and felt like a ghost.

But one day, as I joined my voice with those in the church, I realised I was not a solitary note, trying to be heard. I was part of the music.

Kyrie eleison. Kyrie eleison. Kyrie eleison.

Saying the familiar words carried my mind to a quieter place. I took the host in my mouth and was blessed, and I felt the burden of my soul lift as I became part of the church again.

It was then that I took Sara into my confidence. I asked her to visit the parchment maker for me and bring me offcuts, together with cheap paper, quills and ink. I asked her not to tell anyone that I had requested these items, but promised her that they were to be used for God's work only.

She seemed pleased I had trusted her, and swore to keep my secret as close as her own skin.

MARGERY

Another time I had been in church praying again that I might have a chaste marriage, when Jesus said that if I fasted on Friday from both meat *and* drink, then I would have my wish before Whit Sunday, for he would slay sexual desire in my husband.

This was hard for me to imagine, as my husband was always lusting after my body.

On Whitsun Eve I was at mass in St Margaret's when I heard a thundering noise. I thought that God was taking vengeance on me, as the woman had said. I knelt down with my hands over my head, praying to Our Lord Jesus Christ for mercy, and something hard and heavy thumped on to my back.

I thought my back was broken and feared I would shortly be dead. But when I cried out, 'Jesus, mercy!' the pain was gone. I turned to see what had happened, and a section of the church vault – a chunk of stone and part of the short end of a beam – were on the floor.

A good man, by name of John of Wereham, witnessed this event and feared I was severely injured. He touched my sleeve and asked how I was.

'I am perfectly well!' I told him in all honesty, and indeed I felt no pain at that time nor afterwards.

Then the spirit of the Lord told me in my soul that it was a miracle, and that if I were not believed he would work a great many more for me.

My friend Master Aleyn was most interested to hear about this event, and he fetched both the stone and the beam (which one of the keepers of the church was about to put on a fire) and weighed them. The stone weighed at least three pounds, and the short end of the beam weighed at least six pounds. Master Aleyn said it was a great miracle and he told many people about it.

That evening my brother Ralph came for dinner, with his wife Katherine who everybody said was very beautiful. I told them about the stone that fell on me in church, and the miracle that God did not let me be hurt. Ralph winked at his wife and said he had never heard of God hurling rocks at those he loved, at which she laughed so much she spilt some wine on her kirtle.

JULIAN

One day there was a baptism in the church, and I watched the ceremony from my window. As the holy water was sprinkled on the blessed child, she cried out with all the might of her tiny lungs. I had to lie on my bed, my grief for my own baby was so piercing.

I looked at the wooden crucifix on my wall and tried to think about Jesus Christ's suffering, reminding myself that he was our salvation. And it was while gazing at his precious body that I remembered the words which were said very distinctly to me during my *shewings*.

Not 'You shall not be perturbed.'

Not 'You shall not be troubled.'

Not 'You shall not be distressed.'

But 'You shall not be overcome.'

After that I busied myself, keeping my mind steady with prayer. I learnt to keep a closer hold on my thoughts and not to dwell so much on the past. I continued to think of Simon, but now, instead of fretting, I calmly prayed for his blessed soul.

I was perturbed at times, troubled at times, distressed at times. But I was not overcome.

Soon visitors began to arrive, interested to meet the anchoress of Norwich, to pray with me and receive my counsel. I hid my sorrows and distresses from them, as I listened to theirs. I learnt that human pain varies little.

And then one day I discovered that when I prayed, the walls did not contain me. I prayed and each prayer was a stone removed. I thought of God's love and the walls disappeared.

God is a window through which to see the world.

MARGERY

Soon after this time, at Jesus' behest, I began dressing only in white, giving up all my fine clothes and bright silks and fur trims. When Jesus told me to wear white, I knew my neighbours would laugh, because only chaste women wear white and I now had twelve children torn from my loins. But Jesus told me not to argue, that I should do as I was bid by him who knew best. And he said, 'The more you are ridiculed for the love of me, the more you please me.'

Also, he said that I was a virgin in my soul, and that in heaven I would dance with other holy virgins and he would call me his own beloved darling.

So I said, 'For your love, I shall wear white clothes, even though all the world shall wonder at me.'

Sure enough, the people of Lynn laughed at my white robe, and my husband swore at me for the cost of those other clothes I would no longer wear. He took God's name in vain, which I told him hurt God a great deal.

Also at Our Lord's command, using money given to me for the telling of my visions, I had a ring made that said *Jesus est amor meus*. I wore it secretly on a chain and did not tell my husband.

JULIAN

I have never found it easy to begin speaking. To disturb the silence. Why should I assume that I'll be listened to? Why should anyone assume that their voice, words, song, should fill the mind of another? To displace every other possible sound or word? To displace God?

But writing was different. When I began to write, I felt as though I was speaking to God directly. Yet I also felt that the words came *from* God, that they were his gifts.

If God didn't want me to write, why did the urge blaze in me? For now I had begun to write again, I did not seem to be able to stop.

I was grateful Sara never pressed me about what business a woman had with paper and ink. Indeed, she seemed to regard my privacy as a treasure to watch over, like a dragon with a heap of gold pieces.

I wrote each *shewing* afresh and dwelt on them even when I was not writing about them. I discovered I could go back to them in my mind whenever I wanted, as if they were a place that I could explore and come to know better. What is more, I could talk to Christ and ask him questions and he would speak to me, not with words I could hear, but that formed in my understanding. All the time, Christ was helping me to better understand God's love.

Sometimes I reworked, with much crossing out and burning of papers; I had to sift through my thoughts for words that gleamed with truth. But other times the words came fast, and then I was an arrow, sprung from a bow in God's service.

MARGERY

I sorrowed that my brother Ralph thought God was hurling rocks at me out of hatred instead of love, until Jesus told me, 'You shall be eaten and gnawed by people's talk, just like a rat gnaws the stockfish. But don't be afraid, daughter, for you shall be victorious over all your enemies. I shall give you grace enough to answer every cleric.'

This was proven to be true, for in time I met and answered many clerics. Once I was weeping in the street for Christ's suffering, when a friar said to me, 'Woman, Jesus is long since dead!'

To which I replied, 'Sir, his death is as fresh to me as if he had died this same day, and so, I think, it ought to be to you and to all Christian people.'

He tutted and would speak with me no more, nor let me listen when he preached.

What I wanted more than anything was to travel to the Holy Land (not just in my mind), to see where Jesus had lived and died. I asked my husband if I might make a pilgrimage to Jerusalem but he said no.

He did say I could go to York, though, to see the shrine of St William. So a couple of weeks later, I was in the Chapterhouse of York Minster when a doctor of divinity said to me, 'Woman, what are you doing here in this part of the country?'

I said, 'Sir, I come on pilgrimage here, to honour St William's shrine.'

And he asked me, 'Do you have a husband?'

To which I replied that I did.

'Do you have a letter recording his permission to come here?'

Well, this annoyed me a good deal. 'Sir,' I said. 'My husband gave me permission with his own mouth. Why do you proceed in this way with me more than you do with other pilgrims who are here, and who have no letter any more than I have? Them you let go in peace and quiet, undisturbed, and yet you do not leave me alone!'

I knew that he had heard of my visions and weeping, and that if he could prove I was a heretic, it would look good for him. So I said, 'If there be any cleric here amongst you who can prove that I have said any word otherwise than I ought to, I am ready to put it right very willingly. I will neither maintain error nor heresy, for it is my will entirely to hold as the Holy Church holds, and fully to please God.'

So then this doctor of divinity, and many other worthy clerics, examined me in the Articles of the Faith and on other points as they pleased, all of which I answered well and truly, so that they might have no occasion in my words to harm me, thanks be to God.

Yet despite these answers, the doctor commanded that I should be put in prison, until I could appear before the Archbishop of York. But the secular people gathered round did answer for me, saying that I should not go to prison, for they would themselves go to the Archbishop with me.

And so the doctor and other clerics said no more to me at this time, but let me go wherever I wanted – worship be to Jesus!

JULIAN

During my *shewings* I had walked on the seabed and I returned to this *shewing* in my mind, wandering the sandy hills and valleys. The seaweed undulated in the current, like the hazel tree swaying in the wind outside my window, bowing to the will of God.

It was peaceful below the water, dim and flickery like those moments when we first enter sleep, or first wake, and our mind is dreamy and without fear.

I realised that it was my soul that was walking on the seabed, not my external body; my soul that is the essence of myself that God loves for all time, from when it was first made to eternity.

It is this soul that matters to God. For when we go to church and pray or confess our sins, we think we are presenting our best self to God, and that he is impressed with our tidy robes and clean hands. But God sees past those things, he pays the surfaces of ourselves no heed. He has no interest in the neatness of our stockings or the cleanness of our hems.

He sees that we are weaker and more in need of love than we admit to ourselves.

MARGERY

The next day I was brought into the Archbishop's chapel, and many of the Archbishop's household came to see me, calling me 'Lollard' and 'heretic', and swearing with many horrible oaths, saying that I should be burnt.

My flesh trembled and quaked amazingly, and I was glad I could put my hands under my clothes so that this should not be noticed.

Through the strength of Jesus, I replied to them, 'Sirs, I fear you will be burnt in hell without end, unless you correct yourselves of your swearing of oaths, for you do not keep the commandments of God. I would not swear as you do for all the money in this world.'

Then they went away, as if they were ashamed, and I prayed to God, asking for the grace to behave as would most please him and to profit my own soul. And Our Lord answered me and said that all would go well.

The Archbishop came into the chapel and said to me abruptly, 'Why do you go about in white clothes? Are you a virgin?'

And I knelt before him and said, 'No, sir, I am no virgin; I am a married woman with many children.'

He sent a member of his household to fetch a pair of fetters, and said I should be fettered for I was a false heretic, so I said, 'I am no heretic, nor shall you prove me one.'

Then many worthy clerics arrived, including the doctor of divinity who had interviewed me before. They took their seats according to their degree, and it all took so long that I melted into tears. The Archbishop and his clerics, who had not heard my crying before, were astonished.

The Archbishop spoke crossly, saying, 'Why do you weep so, woman?'

And I replied, 'Sir, you shall wish some day that you had wept as sorely as I.'

He gave me a sour look and began to put to me the Articles of our Faith, as had the other clerics previously, to which God gave me the grace to answer so well and truly that the Archbishop could not criticise me. He said to the clerics, 'She knows her faith well enough. What shall I do with her?'

And they said that even though I knew my Articles of the Faith, I should not be allowed to dwell among them, because the people had great faith in my talk and might be led astray.

Then the Archbishop said, 'I have been told very bad things about you. I hear it said that you are a very wicked woman.'

And I replied, 'Sir, I also hear it said that you are a wicked man. And if you are as wicked as the people say, you will never get to heaven, unless you amend while you are here.'

Then he said very roughly, 'Why you!' I thought he would strike me, but he seemed to gather himself. He asked me what people said about him.

I answered, 'Other people, sir, can tell you well enough.'

Then a cleric in a furred hood stepped forward and said, 'Quiet! Speak about yourself, and let him be.'

After this, the Archbishop made me lay my hand on the book before him and swear that I would leave his diocese as soon as possible, and he gave a man five shillings to escort me.

I got down on my knees and asked the Archbishop's blessing, which he gave me, and then he let me go. But before I left York I was received by many people who rejoiced that the Lord had given me the wit and wisdom to answer so many learned men without shame.

JULIAN

I had been in my cell for some years, when Master Thomas preached a sermon against women who claimed to have visions of God. He also preached against women who taught the word of God, for St Paul had written: *Let women keep silence in the churches; for it is not permitted them to speak, but to be subject.*

I wondered if my secret was known to him and I was afraid lest I be hauled from my cell and accused of heresy. I had never heard of an anchoress's cell being searched, but that didn't mean it couldn't happen. I prayed hard to God that he show me the right path, for I did not want to stray from the teachings of his true Church, but to be orthodox in all things. I wrote again and again in my book: *In all things I believe what the Church teaches.*

MARGERY

My husband and I were returning from another pilgrimage together, this time from Walsingham, when it occurred to me that he had not made love to me for eight weeks, even though I had lain beside him in bed every night for all this time. When we stopped to rest at a wayside cross I asked him the reason and he said, 'I am made so afraid when I go to touch you, that I dare to do it no more.'

It was just as Jesus had promised!

I said, 'I told you that your desire for sex would be slain.'

Then he said, 'Margery, if a man came with a sword and said he would strike off my head unless I made love to you, would you allow my head to be cut off, or would you allow me to make love to you?'

And I said, 'Sir, I would rather see you killed than go back to that uncleanness.'

And he said, 'You are no good, wife.'

JULIAN

One day God offered me a gift through Sara. She brought me a handful of hazelnuts from the tree I could see from my window. I looked at one of the nuts in my hand and asked, 'What can it be?' even though I knew it to be a hazelnut. The answer was given to me immediately: 'It is all that is made.'

As a young woman, every time I sat under the chancel arch in church I had looked at the paintings of sinners being dragged by demons to the mouth of hell – where unfaithful wives were stripped and beaten, money-lenders roasted, and murderers boiled in oil – and I'd wondered why the Lord was so angry with us. I wondered how God could love us, since we were such sinful creatures.

But now, as I looked at the hazelnut nestling in my palm, I understood that all things have being through the love of God. And I was no longer afraid. God was not a tyrant who would see me stripped and burnt; he loved us and nurtured us all as his own dear children.

I remembered being a wife and mother, rinsing the herring for dinner, using a sharp knife to scrape away the scales before hanging the fish above the fire. Days later I'd find scales between the stone flags of the floor, stuck to the wall, caught in my woollen shawl. Now, when I remembered how they were everywhere, I saw that it was just the same with God's love. God is not a being on high, to whom we must raise our eyes. God is everywhere, in all things, including us. We are clad in the goodness of God, so closely that our souls and God are one thing, and that this one-ing is the most important thing to understand. For if we are oned with God, we can never be divided from him.

I thought about sin and how, in my *shewings*, I had seen nothing of sin. And then I realised – that was because sin was nothing. 'Wretched sin!' I called out. 'What are you? You are nothing! I saw that God has made all things, and I saw nothing of you; and when I saw that God is in all things, I saw nothing of you.'

However, I still didn't understand how it could be that we all sinned and yet we would be saved through Christ's love. But then God gave me another thought which eased my mind. There are two kinds of judgement: God judges our natural essence, our soul, which is always preserved unchanged in him, whole and safe for ever; whereas men judge us in terms of our changeable sensory being, which seems now one thing, now another, according to various influences on it and its outward appearance.

So even if Simon died unshriven, his soul was loved by God, and he would be in heaven.

And there our two souls will be joined for all eternity.

MARGERY

My brother Ralph paid my husband a visit to say he would not be bringing his wife into our company any more, for he had heard that I had been accused of heresy by the Archbishop of York. To associate with me had been shaming, but it was now also dangerous.

I was grieved to hear this as I was still fond of my brother. But then I discovered his wife had been spreading rumours about me, encouraging the people of Lynn to laugh at me and denounce me. When I heard that I was glad that I would see no more of my brother, nor his nasty wife.

I enjoyed going into the town less and less, wondering what people were whispering about me. I did not stand by the Guildhall on Tuesdays to share my visions any more, as both Master Aleyn and Master Spryngolde kept reminding me that women were not permitted to preach. Both of these good men knew I *wasn't* preaching, but they suggested it might not be easy to explain to other clerics that I was only having conversation with a crowd of people.

I was also getting more abuse than gratitude from other townsfolk. Once, as I was walking back from the market, a man deliberately threw a bowlful of water on my head. I said to him, 'God make you a good man' and I highly thanked God for it. I said to the Lord that these humiliations were as nothing to me, and that I would, for God's love, be laid naked on a hurdle for all men to wonder at (so long as it were no danger to their souls) and they could throw mud and slime at me, if the Lord was pleased by this.

JULIAN

I worked at my book and I spoke to the people who visited my window and prayed with them. The days and nights swam by. I heard the wind and the rain, and these comforted me.

Before I came to my cell, I had many foolish thoughts: *I am like this, I am not like this. I want that, I do not want that.* My thoughts were sticky and black as treacle: they held me trapped, unable to move forward.

But now
    my mind is clearer
        and I can think
            like a river
                thinks its way
                    between hills
                        or the wind
                            thinks its way
                                through the leafy boughs
                            of a tree

I have become a great watcher of light and dark. Once the golden light of the sun sinks away, the colour is taken out of things, and the world fades one object at a time. First, the opposite street becomes nothing but a shadow. Then the hazel tree picks up blackness. In winter, it forms a tracery of branches and twigs against the gloaming sky; in summer the leaves lose their distinction from one another. Soon you cannot tell what is leaf, and what is brick, and what is cloud obliterating the last remnants of the deepening heavens.

In the morning, I watch the world coming into being, leaf by leaf, brick by brick, cloud by cloud, as if every day God says *Let there be light* and creates the world afresh.

MARGERY

Sometimes, when Jesus appeared to my spiritual sight, I thought him the handsomest man that had ever been seen or imagined.

And once, in the sight of my soul, I saw Our Lord standing right up over me, so near that I took his unsandalled toes in my hand and they felt like flesh and bone. I had intimacy with Christ, his skin on my skin. And then it did not matter so much what Ralph thought, or his wife, or Agnes and her husband, or any other of the neighbours and townsfolk who laughed behind their hands, or called out unkindnesses to my face.

JULIAN

Today the sky is perfectly blue. No sound but a blackbird singing and a bee humming. There are bees that live in my wall, solitary as anchoresses themselves.

When I think of the blue sky, the blackbird's song, the bee, I feel awe.

I wrote in my book: *The soul must perform two duties. One is that we reverently marvel. The other is that we humbly endure, ever taking pleasure in God.*

These two duties guide me.

MARGERY

Jesus said that I would have no other purgatory other than the slanderous talk I endured in this world. So many evil things were said about me, that Jesus said it was a miracle I still had my wits, considering the vexation I suffered.

Indeed, I asked Jesus to allow me into heaven soon, but he told me he had ordained me to kneel before the Trinity to pray, and that many thousands of people would be saved by my prayers.

JULIAN

I watch a yellow-black striped snail make its way along my windowsill. Perhaps, for a snail, it is hurrying; time may be different for a snail.

Time has not been a steady friend to me.

In the early years in my cell, the minutes between the bells ringing out for prayer were so long I used to wonder if the bell was broken or if the bell-ringer was distracted. But now the hours are mere minutes, the days are just hours, and winter approaches before I have even noticed the scent of freshly scythed hay.

MARGERY

I do not think I should like to be old, though I do not care to die either. I asked Jesus about my death, because if I was going to suffer I wanted to know, and also whether great suffering would mean I went to heaven quicker.

I thought I would like to be slain for his sake, though I greatly feared the actual point of death, so I kept imagining easy deaths for myself, such as being tied to a stake and having my head struck off with a sharp axe, for the love of God.

But Jesus said I had nothing to fear from the manner of my death, that no man would slay me, nor would fire burn me, nor water drown me. He said he would not take me before my time and I was not to fret about any pain or suffering because it would be a quiet death. Then he said that he will come to me at my dying, with his blessed mother and the holy angels, and Mary Magdalene, and the twelve apostles.

I was much relieved to hear it, though I should have suffered gladly if it had been his will.

JULIAN

My book is finished and I have a hollow feeling, as if I were an empty hazelnut shell. But I know such feelings do not matter, because I am of no account. I must stand aside and let my book speak.

I had thought that, because I was a woman, I could not tell people that I had seen the goodness of God. But it is clear to me now that my book should go out into the world. For how do we know of the experiences of the disciples, and the saints, and other holy men and women? We know of what they experienced from their words that were written down.

A strange thing happened when I told Sara I did not need any more paper or ink. She said: 'Is it finished?'

'It was just a few scribbles, Sara,' I said. 'It has mostly fed the fire.'

'I will look after it for you,' she said. 'Give it to me.'

In truth, I *had* been thinking I might entrust her with my book, but the way she said it – her voice was like a dagger in my belly.

'Just a few scribbles,' I repeated. 'Nothing that needs to be looked after.'

MARGERY

Despite my bad experiences at York, I was eager to visit many other holy places in England. I wanted to go to Leicester, which I'd heard had many fine churches.

However, the first I went into had a crucifix so piteously portrayed, it was lamentable to behold. As I looked at it, the Passion of Our Lord entered my mind and I began to dissolve with tears of pity and compassion. A man said, 'Woman, why are you weeping so bitterly?'

I did not like this man – I didn't like the cruel look on his face, as if he would slit my throat if he thought he could do so unpunished. So I said, 'Sir, it is not to be told to you.'

Then I went to the inn where I was lodging and while I was having a meal, the innkeeper told me I had to go immediately and speak with the Mayor. This I did, and the Mayor asked me from which part of the country I came, and whose daughter I was.

'Sir,' I said. 'I am from Lynn in Norfolk, the daughter of a good man of the same Lynn, who has been five times mayor of that worshipful borough, and also an alderman for many years; and I have a good man, also a burgess of the said town of Lynn, for my husband.'

'Ah,' said the Mayor. 'St Katherine told of what kindred she came, and yet you are not alike, for you are a false strumpet, a false Lollard, and a false deceiver of the people, and therefore I shall have you in prison.'

To which I replied, 'I am as ready, sir, to go to prison for God's sake, as you are ready to go to church.'

He was not pleased with this reply, and commanded the gaoler's man to lead me to prison. The gaoler's man had compassion for me and said to the Mayor, 'Sir, I have no place to put her, unless I put her in among men.'

And I said, 'I beg you, sir, do not put me among men, so that I may keep my chastity, and my bond of wedlock to my husband.'

And the gaoler's man said to the Mayor, 'Sir, I will undertake to keep this woman in my own safekeeping until you want to see her again.'

I was moved by this man and prayed for grace and mercy for him. And he led me to his own house and put me in a fine room and locked the door, but let me eat at his table, and made me very welcome for Our Lord's love.

Then the Steward of Leicester wanted to interview me so I was sent to him. He spoke in Latin and brought many priests and other people to hear what I would say. I said to him, 'Speak in English, if you please, for I do not understand what you are saying.'

He replied, 'You lie most falsely, to put it in plain English.'

I said, 'Sir, ask what question you will in English, and through the grace of my Lord Jesus Christ I shall answer you very reasonably.'

And then he asked me a great many questions, and these I answered readily and reasonably as I had promised.

But then the Steward took me by the hand and led me into a chamber. He shut the door and stood very close to me. He spoke many foul, lewd words to me, saying I was a disgrace to my sex, and unclean, and that I deserved to be punished. He pressed himself against me and put his thigh between mine and breathed heavily on my neck. I tried to step away, but he gripped me roughly and then I knew he was intending to overcome me. I wept and begged him for mercy as he lifted my kirtle, and I cried out, 'Sir, for the reverence of Almighty God, spare me, for I am a man's wife!'

At this the Steward dropped his arms and said, 'You shall tell me whether you get this talk from God or from the devil, or else you shall go to prison.'

I smoothed my clothing and looked him in the eye, for I suddenly knew that God would not let me be harmed by this man. 'Sir,' I said. 'I am not afraid to go to prison for my Lord's love. I pray you, do as you think best.'

He looked completely astonished, as if I had given him some revelation. He left off all his lewdness, saying, 'Either you are a truly good woman or a truly wicked woman.'

He let me go free from his chamber and then I was led back to the home of the gaoler's man. Soon afterwards, word came that I was to be released, the Mayor saying I could go wherever I wished. But I did not wish to stay in Leicester.

JULIAN

What is stronger than my will?

Many things: the urge of green things to grow; the urge of light to creep beneath the door; the urge of a cut finger to bond and heal.

My will is little, almost nothing.

When the day begins, we say that it is breaking. So with my life. Part of me had to be taken into pieces before I could truly start to live. For in my *shewings* Jesus had said, 'I shall shatter you for your vain passions and your vicious pride; and after that I shall gather you together and make you humble and meek, pure and holy, by oneing you to me.'

My will was broken and I am glad of it. I am only a thing that moves this broom and sweeps the curled leaves and corpses of insects from one side of my cell to the other.

MARGERY

When I returned home, I told my husband about what had happened to me in Leicester. He gave me no kindness or sympathy, but said I was a disgraceful wife, always gallivanting around the country when I should be at home taking care of our children.

'It's a fine thing for a woman to be encouraging intimacy with other men, when she refuses to sleep with her husband. I've a mind to put you in the stocks.'

I ignored him as I knew he wouldn't do such a thing. He needed me to run the household and care for the children.

I spent more time than ever at St Margaret's, praying and speaking with Jesus in my mind. But then I had a vision in which it was the Heavenly Father speaking to me, not his son Jesus.

He said, 'Daughter, I will have you wedded to my Godhead, and you shall live with me without end.'

I kept quiet in my soul and did not answer this, because I was very much afraid of the Godhead; I had no knowledge of the conversation of the Godhead, for all my love and affection were fixed on the manhood of Christ, and of that I did have knowledge and would not be parted from for anything.

I felt very afraid, but the Heavenly Father took me by the hand, and before the Son and the Holy Ghost and the Mother of Jesus and the twelve apostles, he said, 'I take you, Margery, for my wedded wife, for fairer, for fouler, for richer, for poorer, provided that you are humble and meek in doing what I command you to do.'

I took off my wedding ring and put my other ring on my finger in its stead, the one engraved *Jesus est amor meus*. I did not care what my husband thought any more. He said I was a bad wife, but it wasn't true. He was a bad husband, no matter that Agnes said he was a good man and that I shouldn't be such a trial to him.

When Jesus asked me who I should like as my companion in Heaven, I answered Robert Spryngolde, and he asked why not my husband? And I answered that Master Spryngolde had been very good to me, especially about hearing my confession from the beginning of my life so often. Jesus said that Master Spryngolde could be my companion if I wished it, but that my husband and children were also saved, because of the Lord's love for me.

JULIAN

I look at my brown-spotted hands, their swollen knuckles, and see there is not much longer left to me on earth. My body is stiff, as if already preparing itself for the grave. My knees creak and my fingers struggle with my beads. Indeed, Sara gives me broths and mashed turnips, but no meat because my teeth are crumbling.

But I am ready to die, for death comes to all who live. It is as Jesus said: *Unless a grain of wheat fall into the ground and die, it abideth alone; but if it die, it bringeth forth much fruit.* I do not wish to remain a solitary grain of wheat.

As I listen to my thoughts, I am aware of their repetitive nature, as if my mind was the sea and my thoughts the same wave rolling in.

I think more and more about what to do with my book now that it is complete. The thought of giving it to Sara frightens me. I am dependent on her for a great deal, and grateful, truly. She has made me the centre of her world. But she sometimes treats me as a child. Or as her own possession.

My book needs to be shared with the world, and I trust to God to give me a sign.

MARGERY

Robert Spryngolde says there are so many against me that he fears there is only him and the stars and the moon on my side. But Christ says that one day those few of my neighbours that are permitted into heaven will see me sitting beside God as the most beloved of all the saints, and doted on by Jesus and his blessed mother too.

Jesus says to me, 'Though all the world be against you, don't be afraid, for they cannot understand you.' And he says that if it were possible for him to suffer pain as he had before, he would rather suffer all that pain again, for the sake of my soul alone.

Master Robert says that God deals with me like a smith does a file: he makes the iron bright and clear, which at first seemed rusty and dark; the sharper God is with me, the brighter my soul shines. Therefore I must accept the slander and lies of my neighbours with grace, for it is doing my soul good.

But he also asks me why I do not spend more time at home and care for my children, for God has made me a mother and so I should perform that task as well as I can. I do not know what to say when he tells me that. For the truth is that often I cannot bear to look upon my children, each of whom was torn violently from my own body, with much pain and blood and vomit and other foul substances.

I have been feeling much alone, so I went to my friend Master Aleyn and asked him to read to me again from the life of Bridget of Sweden. Really, our lives are so much alike! She bore many children and went on pilgrimages and managed to convince her husband to live a chaste life. Then she moved to Rome where she founded a new order of nuns and dictated her revelations. They have made her a saint now.

JULIAN

Midwinter. Night crushes day between her fingers, squeezing the light out of her.

A cold thin moon rises, a slip of paper between stars.

The churchyard is silenced by frost, it stills every movement of grass and twig. There is no birdsong, no rustling or squeaking, not even the sound of footsteps in the street.

My cat's eyes gleam in the candlelight, more devil than angel. But then he washes himself, before turning and turning his soft body into a coil, readying himself for the sleep that is so much like death, but from which we all hope to wake each day.

I do not know if it is my age, or if the world gets colder with every winter. Sometimes I cannot feel my fingers or toes. Sara tells me there is ice on the river and boats cannot get through.

MARGERY

I have so many holy thoughts, holy speeches and high revelations, that it is difficult to tell of them or even to remember them all. I wish that I could write them down, as St Bridget and Marguerite Porete did.

But also I fear the devil is dallying with my thoughts. Just as I have had many glorious visions and high contemplations upon the Lord, so I am having many horrible visions recently. I see various men of religion coming before my eyes so that I cannot avoid them or put them out of my sight, showing me their naked genitals. And the devil orders me to choose which of them I will have first, and says that I must prostitute myself to them all.

Whenever I try to look upon the sacraments or say my prayers or do any good deed, such abominations are put into my mind.

I am constantly shriven but I can find no release, and I am nearly in despair. It cannot be written what pain I feel and what sorrow I have. And I say, 'Lord, for thy great pain have mercy on my little pain! Alas, Lord, you have said before that you would never forsake me. Where now is the truthfulness of your word?'

JULIAN

This morning there is a lid of ice on my water jug and the spider above my crucifix is frozen.

I am readying myself for the end of my life. It is only a transition, of course, not truly an end.

I am not afraid of death now it is so close at hand. Just one or two steps and it will hold me. I won't struggle.

MARGERY

It's so cold I think my eyeballs will ice over. I huddle by the fire like a crone. I don't even like going to church because the wind whistles through the nave and puts icicle fingers down my neck.

But if I don't go to church I don't see anybody except my children. No one visits me at home. My father is elderly, my mother is now dead. My brother Ralph will not see me. My husband knows that all the love and affection of my heart is withdrawn from him and set on God alone.

Just yesterday, John said, 'It is your own fault, Margery, that you are a laughing stock. I wish to God I'd never married you, for hardly anyone will do trade with me.'

He has never said such harsh words to me before. I defended myself, saying, 'Jesus showed himself to me that I might tell the world about his love.'

He laughed. 'You talk because you are a woman, not because you have instruction from Jesus. All women talk too much. Your bodies are wetter, so your tongues slip around your mouths more easily.'

I did not listen to any more of his cruel jibes, but went directly to St Margaret's to pray and speak with Robert Spryngolde. He is a very good priest; he has always counselled me to follow the promptings and stirrings of my mind, for he insists they are from the Holy Ghost and not from an evil spirit. But how does he know?

I visit Master Aleyn every week, asking his learned views on my conversations with Jesus, and he never tires of giving me spiritual guidance. He also advises me of other holy persons that I can speak to, and today he told me about Dame Julian, an anchoress in Norwich, who lives an exemplary life. He said that many visit her for her good counsel and that, if I can't rest easy, despite his and Master Spryngolde's assurances that my visions are from God, then perhaps Dame Julian can help me.

I hope so.

If not, I long that I will soon be delivered from this wretched world.

PART TWO

THE MEETING

DAY 1

MARGERY

When I set out for Norwich I felt such hope that my visit to the anchoress would ease my spiritual pains. But as I travelled east my mood sank. The land we rode through was very drab and I could not in all honesty have called those cabbage fields splendid.

Norwich itself is grey and stinks of fish; there are many people bustling around and they all seem to be foreigners, so strange are their robes and voices.

There are some fine ladies, but their headdresses are most astonishing: they have delicate gold piping on top of their heads, bent this way and that to form elaborate patterns in front of their wimples. I have always held my own among the ladies of Lynn, and I do not like the way these women looked at me.

I told my maidservant to stay close, and scold her if she strays out of reach.

Also, there is so much noise in Norwich — the clattering of carts and hooves on stone, the jangling of church bells, the shouts of traders, not to mention the animals braying and whinnying and barking and snorting. No, Norwich does not have the charm of Lynn, nor its fresh sea breezes.

When I reached Dame Julian's cell, I stood at her window and was flayed by a bitter wind from the north. Her stone box was so much like a casket, I shivered all the more.

I could not look upon the anchoress because she kept her curtain drawn, and it trembled in the constant breeze. But when I heard her voice, low and soft like a dove or a dairy cow, I knew she was a most holy person.

JULIAN

Her voice swanned and preened and boasted, yet there was another note to her song. Margery Kempe was the loneliest woman I had ever met.

I took a deep breath and thought how I could best give love to this woman.

§

MARGERY: Dame Julian. It is Margery Kempe from Lynn. I've come to speak with you.

JULIAN: Welcome, daughter.

[A breath of wind passes through the leaves in the hazel tree]

MARGERY: Oh ... I mean ... How to begin? I've visited many anchorites. I've had tea with the Archbishop of York.

JULIAN: Is that what you came here to tell me?

MARGERY: No! It isn't. I ... I wish I could see your face. No, I'm not asking to, I understand you must stay hidden. It's just ... Oh dear. Thank you for allowing me to talk with you. I've heard much of your good counsel.

JULIAN: I will speak with anyone who comes to my window. Tell me, child. Why did you come here to see me? What do you wish to say? You have many thoughts, many words, I can feel them. Let them pour out, and do not be afraid.

MARGERY: Thank you, oh thank you. I hardly know how to begin. I have visions, you see. Jesus comes and sits with me in person. I mean, I know it's a vision in my mind, but it's the same as if he is with me bodily. He even holds my hand!

But I'm afraid ... I worry these are not holy visions.

JULIAN: Does Jesus speak to you in these visions?

MARGERY: Sometimes. And sometimes I see myself ... I see myself at his birth, at his dying, at his resurrection. And I see the Holy Mother and the twelve apostles and Mary Magdalene too, and I comfort them in their sorrow.

Is it heresy to say these things?

[The wind blows harder through the tree]

JULIAN: They sound like holy visions indeed.

MARGERY: But I'm making it sound all wrong. It isn't *just* that Christ is with me and speaks to me. He gives me so much grace and we have such holy conversations – he teaches me how I should love God and worship and serve him. But these things he tells me, they aren't in words. I can't express them with my bodily tongue in the same way that I felt them.

JULIAN: You understand these blessings that the Lord gives you better in your soul than you can utter them to others?

MARGERY: Yes, exactly! But when I try to explain that to others, they say I was never given these teachings or blessings at all. And then I doubt it, too. And many people – who are my neighbours and family and should love me and show me great kindness – they say that I'm lying, or that evil spirits put them in my head.

JULIAN: You tell others of your visions? Are you afraid? Have you been threatened?

MARGERY: Oh, many times. Archbishops and doctors of divinity have fettered me and questioned me night and day, and I have had attacks upon my person and my chastity. But no, these things don't frighten me.

JULIAN: You are a woman of great grace and courage. And though you may suffer much from the words of others, remember that no man may know your heart. God alone knows it.

MARGERY: So do you think they're visions from God? Because you're a most wise and holy woman and I will believe what *you* tell me.

JULIAN: I believe that whenever we are urged to act with compassion, this is God at work in us. If your visions urge you to love and be charitable, then they are visions from God.

MARGERY: But even if they are from God, they do not please people. My friends say, 'Why *you*, Margery? Why are you so special?' And I cannot answer them. All of my neighbours are laughing at me, they even throw things at me in the street for their own amusement. Nobody will visit any more, not even my brother. My husband is tired of me, so there is nobody who loves me.

JULIAN: You are loved by God, Margery.

MARGERY: I am loved by God.

            [A street vendor calls out 'hot peascods!']

JULIAN: I know that you are suffering. But when we die, all will be revealed to us, and then we won't wish anything that happened on earth to have been otherwise.

MARGERY: This is what Jesus tells me too. He says every bit of suffering I have now, will become glory and joy to me in heaven. I pray it will be so, for I suffer so greatly I can hardly stand to live.

JULIAN: There was a time in my life when I also no longer wanted to live.

MARGERY: You, Dame Julian? But you are so famous and beloved.

JULIAN: It was a long time ago, before I made my vows and came to live in this cell.

MARGERY: How did you get through such a time?

JULIAN: God told me that all things would be well. He told me to take my sorrow and pain lightly, for they would pass; indeed, sorrow only lasts for an atom of time compared to all the time when we will be with him and surrounded by his love.

MARGERY: Sorrow feels very long to me.

JULIAN: When we suffer, we are blinded. But believe me when I tell you this. It is what God wants all Christians to know. All shall be well, and all shall be well, and all manner of things shall be well.

MARGERY: I wish I could believe *that*.

But I know I'll feel a lot better when I'm in heaven, and Jesus is there, and his mother, and all the saints, and they're all full of their love for me.

JULIAN: Love for you, and for *all* Christians.

MARGERY: Yes. And there was another thing I wished to ask you about, Dame Julian.

JULIAN: Tell me, child.

MARGERY: As well as visions, I can't stop weeping. Sometimes it is because I'm so tired – I have fourteen children, so I'm usually tired – but also I cannot think of Christ's Passion without weeping. I weep so loudly that people tut and say there is a devil in me. They say I should be turned out of sermons because I'm disrupting the preacher and they can't hear his words.

JULIAN: When God visits a creature with tears of contrition, devotion or compassion, she ought to believe that the Holy Ghost is in her soul. No evil spirit may give these tokens, for St Jerome says that tears torment the devil more than do the pains of hell.

MARGERY: I am glad you think so, Dame Julian, because sometimes I fear the Lord has forsaken me. You see, I cannot help but think of all the times I have offended against the Lord's goodness. I fear I am going to hell, because I can never be worthy of all the suffering the Lord went through for us.

JULIAN: My child, there is no hell. God is love.

MARGERY: But what if I'm damned?

JULIAN: You will be enfolded in God's love.

MARGERY: But if God sees and knows all the secrets of my heart, then he knows of my wickedness.

JULIAN: God is all merciful; remember that he is our mother as well as our father. Think of when your own children fall and hurt themselves. When they are in need of love and care, to whom do they turn? To you, their mother. Now that you are in need of love and care, you should turn to God who loves you without end, like a mother. He wants to comfort you. All he wants from us is our love.

MARGERY: But what if I do not deserve God's love? What if I am not a good mother?

JULIAN: Then return home to your children and *be* a good mother. Remember, every action, every breath, can be the worship of God. Marvel at this world he gave us, and be humble. But above all else, be compassionate. If you have fourteen children, you are blessed indeed.

MARGERY: No, I think you are better off, Dame Julian. You have more freedom in your little room than I ever have, with constant demands for food and clothes and attention. I envy you your lack of children.

JULIAN: Value whatever blessings you have, child. No one knows the sorrow and pain of others.

MARGERY: I've heard that there are orders of monks and nuns who lacerate themselves and use scourges and hair shirts to bring themselves closer to Jesus, to understand his suffering and to speed their souls to him. I wonder if I should mortify my flesh more often – would that help secure my place in heaven?

JULIAN: I do not think that is what he requires of us. Do not mortify yourself, daughter. He died so we are saved. He died because he loves us.

MARGERY: But how do we thank him? With fornicating, envying, lying, boasting, and neglecting our children! I cannot bear to think of the burnings and boilings and whippings that go on in hell.

JULIAN: What is our sin to God who knows everything and exists in eternity? It is nothing. A speck. He can blow – *pfffff* – and it is gone. God is so wide that he is everywhere, and yet he is also in the smallest things – in hazelnuts and fish scales and raindrops. He is everywhere. Sin does not matter to him. Love him, Margery. Let yourself love him as he loves you. Without end.

Now go. Pray and rest. But return to me tomorrow before you leave the city, for I would like to speak with you one more time.

[The wind sends a few green leaves tumbling to the ground]

§

MARGERY

When Dame Julian uttered these words from behind her black curtain, I felt like reaching through it to kiss her hand. I had never felt so utterly comforted (except when Christ comforted me himself, of course).

She will surely be made a saint, she was so kind to me.

JULIAN

I was glad she seemed to take comfort from my words. I said she could come again and speak with me the next day, something I never usually encourage. But this woman ... Her *shewings* are so like my own, seeing Christ's Passion and knowing his words without speech. I've never heard anyone speak of experiences so similar to my own. Then it came to me, like a final *shewing*. A vision of what I would do.

MARGERY

After visiting Dame Julian, the city suddenly felt a more welcoming place, as if a warm sun had emerged. First I went to the market and chose some treats for my children and ordered a roll of fine worsted wool for myself. Now even the inn where I was staying seemed a more pleasing prospect. I rested there awhile, before enjoying some very good creamed fish, followed by mutton stew. The company was most jolly, as some travelling musicians had arrived at the inn, and they played some tunes for us while we ate.

I wondered at Dame Julian, at her constant solitude. Did she ever yearn to be among people – to sing and dance or to simply stroll around the city?

I slept well that night after giving thanks to Jesus for bringing me to the wise anchoress of Norwich.

DAY 2

JULIAN

Before Margery arrived, I was visited by my priest, Father Thomas. He knew that she had been to see me, and said that if the Bishop found out there would be trouble for us both. He told me that many learned men had said that the devil worked through that woman.

I replied that I would receive anyone who wished to speak with me.

'You should not receive heretics,' he told me. 'It casts a pall of suspicion over your own head. If the Bishop comes to hear of it – and he may well ask me about those whom you receive at your cell window – he will want to question you very carefully.'

'Question me?'

'About what is said at your window and about what your own views are.'

'I am faithful to the teachings of the church.'

'So you say. But what *I* say to you is this. Be careful. And be particularly careful about your visitors.'

§

JULIAN: Thank you for coming to my window once more, child. I have my own reasons for wishing to see you again. By your example you give me courage. You speak of your visions even in these dangerous times. People are burnt as heretics for saying less than that they have seen Christ himself. And yet you are not afraid.

I wonder if you would help me, daughter? If you would be fearless on my behalf?

MARGERY: I would be most glad to.

JULIAN: There is something very precious to me that I would like to give you.

MARGERY: Dame Julian, your words are all I need. I admit I used to care about jewels and furs, but now, although you cannot see me, I dress in plain white clothes and wear only one ring, which is engraved with my love for Jesus. People give me coins so that I will pray for them, but I give it all – well, most of it – to the Church.

JULIAN: It's not jewels or furs or gold I wish to give you. And you would be helping me by accepting this gift.

MARGERY: To think a poor creature like me should ever be of service to you!

JULIAN: It's a dangerous gift.

MARGERY: Oh. What do you mean by dangerous?

JULIAN: If it's discovered in your possession, you may be accused of heresy.

MARGERY: I'm accused of heresy every day of my life.

JULIAN: You are a brave woman, Margery Kempe. I admire you.

This thing I wish to give you – it's a book.

MARGERY: A book? Oh. I have long yearned to read and write, but cannot do either. But my good friend Master Aleyn will read it to me, I'm sure.

JULIAN: No, do not ask your friend to read it. Don't
            tell anyone you have it. Just keep it safe. But
            one day, you must share it with the world. I
            believe God will let you know the right time.

MARGERY: What kind of book is it? It's not an English
            Bible is it? I am no Lollard.

JULIAN: It is not a Bible, no. It is my own book, writ-
            ten by myself in English, poor unlettered
            creature that I am.

MARGERY: A book you wrote yourself? What does it say?

JULIAN: It tells of something I saw many years ago.
            Since that time, I have been putting my
            thoughts into ink. These pages are not the
            work of moments but of years, layered to-
            gether as I have striven to understand what
            I saw.

MARGERY: Of something you saw? What was it?

            [A blackbird sings from the hazel tree]

JULIAN: I have never spoken of this to anyone. But I
            am close to the end of my life in this world,
            and God wishes me to share it. That is why
            he gave me the gift of writing.

MARGERY: But what did you see?

JULIAN: It is very hard for me to say out loud. Forgive me, child. I am not as courageous as you. For so many years I have kept this inside me. I wish I had been more like you and spoken of it from the start.

MARGERY: I know what you saw! You saw what I see!

JULIAN: My dear child. I'm so ashamed. I have encased myself in fear.

MARGERY: I will take your book for you. I'll take care of it and never tell a single soul, not even Master Robert or Master Aleyn. I will keep it safe, and share it with the world when it is safe, as you have instructed. May the Lord be my guide.

JULIAN: It is as if I always knew that you would come and take this burden from me. The Lord have mercy on you.

§

JULIAN

I slid the papers, tied up with a rope of silk threads, under the curtain. Margery Kempe reached out to take the bundle but, as she did so, her fingers touched mine. It took all my wits not to cry out – no other person's flesh had touched mine for twenty-three years. Her fingers were soft, without calluses, and her nails were smooth and rounded.

In that moment I glimpsed a strange white scar, as though her hand had once been bitten very hard by a human mouth.

MARGERY

The papers slid out from under the black curtain and I saw her fingers, crabbed like any old woman's. I touched them, as if by accident, and they were dung-dry. I whispered my thanks and left her window immediately, as she had instructed me, hiding the precious papers in my sleeves.

JULIAN

Never have I met such an undaunted woman as Margery Kempe. No threats touch her. She is surely under God's protection.

I sent Sara to fetch Master Thomas, so I might confess the accidental touching of flesh. He seemed impatient with me, as if I was just an old woman wasting his time.

'An accident isn't a sin,' he snapped. 'Say five paternosters and forget about it.'

But I can't forget. My flesh feels seared, as if those hot fingers are on my skin still. It has unsettled me, and now I yearn more than ever to be embraced.

I know God always intended me to give Margery Kempe my book, and that no harm will come to it. Sara may be angry, but it is too late now. I will face her and endure what comes.

With my book in the world, I am free to die. It is to God's embrace that I now turn.

PART THREE

THE BOOKS

MARGERY

It has been several months since my visit to the wise anchoress of Norwich. The journey home was dull with much rain. When I arrived in Lynn at last, saddle-sore and soaked, I was more pleased than I expected to be home again. I gathered my children around me and gave them the sweet treats I'd bought for them. They kissed my cheeks and cried out, 'Mama!' with delight.

I took Dame Julian's pages to my chamber and placed them in a wooden box, wrapped in one of my old linen slips, where they could rest without fear of discovery.

Every day I take the pages out. I study their markings and finger the paper until it grows soft. I press the pages to me, even kiss them. Once I slept with them under my pillow. These are good words, holy words, and God wants me to have them.

Since I saw Dame Julian, I have not felt shame scald my heart in the way it used to. I no longer feel the need to mortify my flesh, or fast for so long, or kneel at prayer for so many hours. And I try to love my children better, though I think wearing a hair shirt might be an easier path to heaven.

Not long after I returned to Lynn, my beloved father died. I miss him deeply, but in his dying he set me free. He left me money, and I paid off my husband's debts in exchange for his permission to travel to Jerusalem. Indeed, he is most gentle with me now, for I have saved him from much financial embarrassment.

When I look at Dame Julian's papers, I wonder what it is to write. What does it mean to record one's passing thoughts, rendering them in ink, so they can whisper themselves into another's mind?

Last week, Jesus spoke to me in my mind again, and said that I should write my own book, for by my writing down my visions, many a man would turn to him and be saved.

I said to my husband that I wished to make a record of my life. 'The words froth inside my brain,' I told him. 'They buzz like bees. I murmur them to myself.'

'But Margery, there would be no interest in such a thing. A woman knows little of life,' he said.

'Other women may be interested,' I said. 'After all, I am well travelled and not everyone has had the good fortune to speak with Dame Julian.'

'Women cannot read,' he said. 'Their brains are too soft.'

But he is wrong. Dame Julian's words can be read by those with the skill, and I will find a way to share them and not let them die like her body. For yes, the news has reached Lynn that Dame Julian has passed to the mercy of Our Lord. My heart is grieved as though an axe had flown through the air and cut a cleft into it.

But if there are words, there is no death. And I *will* write a book of my own. My words will live also. I will tell my story, not to commend myself, but only to show the goodness of our merciful Lord Jesus Christ. And if I am known as a good woman who had holy visions and who is later worshipped as a saint, then that is God's will. Amen.

EPILOGUE

After the death of her father, Margery travelled widely as a pilgrim, visiting Rome, Assisi, Jerusalem and Santiago de Compostela, sharing her visions and weeping 'most copiously', to the annoyance of her fellow pilgrims.

She never learnt to read or write, but in her sixties she dictated her story to a scribe — initially to her eldest son, John, who had lived abroad so long that his written English was rather poor; and subsequently to a priest, who tried to improve on John's efforts. Because she was illiterate, Margery cannot have checked what was written and how true the scribe was to the words she spoke, yet a distinctive voice comes singing from the pages of *The Book of Margery Kempe* — the voice of a woman who is boastful, troubled, scorned and lonely. It's the voice of a real human being, telling her story in a rambling fashion but giving deep insight into the life of a medieval woman of the merchant class. A woman about whom we usually hear nothing in the annals of history. But she was never made a saint.

The book that Margaret Kempe dictated is the first autobiography written in English by a man or woman. *The Book of Margaret Kempe* was lost for many centuries, although its existence was known through seven pages of extracts that had been printed in 1501 by Wynkyn de Worde, who incorrectly described her as an anchoress.

In 1934, a fifteenth-century manuscript (not the original, but a near-contemporary copy) fell out of the cupboard in a country house when a guest was looking for a ping pong ball. It was *The Book of Margery Kempe*.

Revelations of Divine Love by Julian of Norwich is the earliest surviving book in English written by a woman. It is in two sections – the Short Text, possibly written not long after she experienced her sixteen *shewings* in 1373, and the Long Text, probably written during her years as an anchoress (between the 1380s and at least 1416).

It's not known how *Revelations of Divine Love* was smuggled out of Julian's cell – if it was found after her death it would probably have been destroyed – but it's possible she gave it to Margery Kempe, who visited her in 1413. Afterwards, it was preserved by a succession of women, including an order of English Benedictine nuns at Cambrai in France. When the nuns were persecuted during the French Revolution and fled to England, Julian's book was lost again. Like *The Book of Margery Kempe*, the original manuscript of *Revelations of Divine Love* is missing, but three copies of the Long Text, possibly made by the nuns in their convent at Cambrai, survive.

These two books, both so nearly lost for ever, are two of the most important books written in the medieval period – and they are both by women.

ACKNOWLEDGEMENTS

For having faith in this book and thereby utterly changing my life, a huge thank you to Sam Copeland and Allegra Le Fanu.

Thanks also to everyone at RCW and Bloomsbury who has helped to bring this book to fruition, including Elisabeth Denison, Charlotte Norman, Helen Francis, brilliant cover designer Carmen Balit, and all those who work to make books a reality and to share them with readers.

To those individuals and organisations that have supported my writing over the years, thank you from the bottom of my heart. This includes: the Scottish Book Trust, especially Lynsey Rogers and Will Mackie; Ruth Thomas; Robert Crawford; Cove Park; Rebecca DeWald; the late and much missed Jennie Erdal; Varuna, the National Writers' House, especially Amy Sambrooke, Veechi Stuart and Carol Major; Creative Scotland; Moniack Mhor, especially Rachel Humphreys and Cynthia Rogerson; The Bridge Awards; Janice Galloway; Hawthornden Literary Retreat; the Oppenheim-John Downes Memorial Trust and Saari Residence (The Kone Foundation).

For advice and reading suggestions, thank you to Lesley Hirst, Charlotte Clutterbuck and Laura Varnum. For reading parts of my manuscript and offering advice and encouragement, thank you to everyone on the Varuna-Cove Park Lamplight Residency in July 2020, especially Lauren Mackenzie.

For love and support, thank you to my family, especially Mum, Dad, Holly, Laura, Annette and Alistair. Thanks to my lovely pals — Jona, Heather, Rachel, Karen W, Karen H, Kirsti W and Adele. An especial thank you to my dear friend Wendy Stedman — without your steady encouragement over the last two decades, I wouldn't be a writer at all.

And finally — thank you to Garry. Without you, there would be no book, and not much anything else. You are my everything.

A NOTE ON THE AUTHOR

Victoria MacKenzie is a fiction writer and poet. She has won a number of writing prizes, including a Scottish Book Trust New Writers Award, and has been awarded writing residencies in Scotland, Finland and Australia.

victoriamackenzie.net
@forthygreatpain

A NOTE ON THE TYPE

The text of this book is set in Perpetua. This typeface is an adaptation of a style of letter that had been popularised for monumental work in stone by Eric Gill. Large scale drawings by Gill were given to Charles Malin, a Parisian punch-cutter, and his hand-cut punches were the basis for the font issued by Monotype. First used in a private translation called 'The Passion of Perpetua and Felicity', the italic was originally called Felicity.